The Black Iris

The Adventures of Silver Dove, Book Four

Eliza Scalia

Cover Illustration by:
Wayne F. Shurtz and Cheyanne and Jean
Buffkin
Based upon the characters originally
designed by Suji Gallianetti

Dedicated to Amanda West for giving me guidance on the subject of autism and providing feedback. She is an Ambassador for Autism in Tennessee, but more importantly, she is a mother of a wonderful boy with autism. This is also dedicated to an old friend who also shared in this struggle, although we left each other on the wrong foot, I miss you and your family, I hope you are happy.

Chapter One
Colomba-
Alone in
the Crowd

Sitting on the bus to start another day of school, I sit alone as I wait for Nat to get picked up. More than anything I want this bus to hurry and reach her stop. I feel everyone's eyes on me as they talk about me just like everybody else in school. Their whispers seem to echo in my head while they spread lies about me. I stare out the window, but I don't really see anything as I try to avoid seeing them looking at me.

It has been almost two weeks since I stopped the Sprinter from attacking the school, and that is also when all of the rumors spreading about me started. Before I transformed into Silver Dove to save the day, a bunch of rocks had covered my leg, trapping me, and the Crow had saved me. A bunch of people saw him carrying me to safety and now everyone thinks that I am partnered up with the Crow, some people even think that I'm dating him. Most people have been avoiding me like I'm a diseased rat or something and talking about me behind my back. As I feel their glares beating down on me, I feel my body slouch, as if I am a wilting flower. I look out the window again to try and pretend they're not there. Ps, it doesn't work very well.

Countless people have tried to come up and talk to me about what happened with the Crow. They all said that they wanted to hear the truth and I told them all the truth. The problem is that none of them seem to have believed me since the rumors have still spread despite how many people I have talked to about this. Everything seems so hopeless right now. One of the only people who is still standing by my side is Nat. Nat has always stood by me, and I have always stood by her. No matter what has happened we always stick with each other. That is why she is my best friend. Something is bothering me though. Luis has been avoiding me since this started happening too.

Out of all my friends, I never would have thought that Luis would abandon me if I started getting bullied. Apparently I was wrong. I have always thought Luis had been picked on too, so I didn't think he would care about this and he would stay by my side. What really surprises me is that he seems to be avoiding me because of a rumor about the Crow. He has always supported the Crow, so why is he avoiding me when everyone thinks that I am helping him? Wouldn't he be happy about all of that? Wouldn't he be happy to think that I'm joining the Crow's side like he's always wanted? I don't understand any of this. Boys are so confusing.

My heart aches when I think of Luis. I want him here with me. I miss him. I miss all of the strange, funny stories he told us. I miss how he was always there for me when I needed him. And I miss how he would always smile when he saw me. I push away the thoughts of Luis so that I won't get completely depressed. It is hard to do but I manage to do it. I've had a lot of practice trying to not think about Luis over the past few weeks.

In what feels like ages, Nat finally comes on the bus and my first little bit of happiness of the day brings a smile to my face. The colorful beads in her braided hair bounce with each step she takes as she makes her way toward me. I notice that several people give her a death glare when they see her sitting with me. She either doesn't notice or is trying not to care about their mean thoughts. One more reason why I absolutely love Nat.

"Hi Nat." She notices the gloominess hidden behind my smiling face and gives me a hug to try and cheer me up.

"Hey Birdy, is everybody still acting like you got the plague?" I can't help but chuckle at her words. No matter how bad I am feeling she can always make me laugh.

"Yeah, no matter what I say or do everyone just keeps avoiding me." She pats me on the back, trying to comfort me in my distress.

"Don't worry. I'm sure that these rumors will die out soon."

"That's what you said over a week ago and it just seems to be getting worse. I don't think that this will ever get better." She wraps her arm around my shoulder and gives me a warm smile.

"Don't worry." She repeats. "Everything will be alright. I just know it will." We chat with each other as the bus continues along its way, but I'm not really that into the conversation. My mind is still stuck on the angry looks people keep giving us every now and again. When the bus stops at Luis' place, I look at the front of the bus. I hope to see him come on, but I don't see him at all. My heart sinks a little further down into my stomach as I try to continue the conversation with Nat, but I really just listen to her as she speaks. I am no longer in the mood to talk.

Everything seems to pass by me as we make our way to school. I wish the bus could just take me home. I want to just curl up under my covers and go back to sleep. I don't want to go through the doors of that school again to have everyone stare and point at me.

As the bus pulls in front of the school, I step off the bus and start heading inside. I'm hoping that everything will be alright today. Glancing around at the people around me, I notice one person that brings a small smile to my face, Cheyanne. She was the one who had been possessed by the Crow not too long ago and she became the Sprinter. Everyone was making fun of her because she is the star of the track team and she broke her leg not too long before a big track competition and they all treated her as if she had betrayed them. Now she is back to her normal self and is hanging out with better people, not like the friends she used to have on the track team who turned on her when she needed them the most. I feel a bit better, knowing that I helped her, but that good feeling doesn't last very long.

Somewhere close to me, I hear someone whispering my name along with a few other mean words. I lower my eyes to the ground and quickly walk inside. They all think that I am trying to help the Crow destroy this school. They are all afraid of me, but more than that, they hate me. I can feel their hatred coming from all of them. They want me to leave the school just as much as I do. If only I could just stay away from all of them. If only all of these terrible rumors would just go away.

Chapter Two
Luis-
Avoiding

As soon as I stepped onto the bus I practically leapt into the first seat on the bus to make sure that Colomba and Nat wouldn't see me get on. I can't let them see me. I can't have them trying to come up and talk to me. I need to avoid them the best that I can. A few weeks ago, I had tripped Alex as he was chasing me so that he landed in a mud puddle. He was covered in mud from head to toe and everyone laughed at him. It felt great at the moment, but I have regretted it ever since. Ever since then I have been waiting for him to get his revenge on me. No matter what Alex always gets his revenge. It has been awful waiting for him. I just want him to get it over with so I can get back to my regular life. I have been having to avoid Colomba ever since I realized that Alex will hurt her if she gets involved in whatever it is that he has planned. I know that if she sees what Alex is doing to me, then she will try to stop Alex and he wouldn't forgive her for siding with me instead of him. So, to keep her safe, I have had to avoid her. It is killing me. It's hard to avoid the only real friends you've ever had.

I'm surprised that Alex hasn't done anything to me yet. It has been like three weeks or so since that happened. Why hasn't he done anything yet? I know that he has something up his sleeve though. He hasn't done anything to me for a while now, which is weird by itself, but when he looks at me he has that evil little look in his eyes that tells me that he has something planned for me. I get a chill down my spine every time I see that look. I want to just stay home and avoid him, but I need to let this happen or else it will never end. Just get it over with and things will go back to normal. That's what I keep telling myself. I've dealt with him getting revenge on me before, I can do it again.

Once he and a bunch of his friends dragged me into a farm field near the middle school I used to go to with him and they threw me onto a pile of cow manure. That was at the beginning of the day, so I had to spend the entire school day smelling like I had bathed in a toilet. He did that to me just because I said hi to the girl he was dating at the time. The problem right now though is that Alex seems to be enjoying keeping me in suspense. He knows that the waiting is torture for me, and he has always enjoyed seeing me in pain. The creep.

Even though I haven't been able to hang out with Colomba recently because of Alex, that hasn't stopped me from hearing the rumors being spread about her right now. Everyone thinks that she is helping me out as the Crow since they saw me save her from getting her leg crushed by those rocks. I smile when I think of that. Maybe since I saved her she will start thinking of the Crow in a different way. Maybe she will join my side. Who knows? Even though that is nice for me to think about I can't forget that that is the only bright side to what is going on right now. She is constantly being hurt by people and everyone is avoiding her. It is really painful for me to just watch this happen to her, knowing that I can't really do anything. Just like with everything else in my life, I am completely powerless.

The bus stops in front of the school and I move quickly so that I am the first one out and I run to the front doors to make sure that Colomba and Nat won't see me and try to talk to me. As I make it through the front doors I hear someone say a familiar name and I turn my attention to them.

"Yeah, Colomba is definitely siding with the Crow. I heard from Angela that Colomba is dating the Crow and that we need to stay away from her as much as we can so that we won't get hurt." The girl that person is talking to shakes their head in disbelief.

"I can't believe that Colomba would side with a lunatic like the Crow. I mean, she seems so nice." The other person chuckles at their friend as if they are being stupid.

"Yeah, it's probably just a really good disguise. Make everyone think that you're an angel when you're really a demon on the inside. I bet that's what it is. One day she'll show her true colors and I can tell you now, it will be frightening. Only a monster would side with another monster." I glare at that person as they continue to walk down the hallway, but they don't see me. I am invisible to them just like how I'm invisible to everyone else.

I want to transform into the Crow right now and create a bunch of my demon dogs to make them regret what they just said, but I know I can't. I can't just use my powers to hurt people who upset me. I need to remember my mission. I am here to end the bullying in my school, not hurt people. Transform enough of the bullied kids into superpowered people and have them scare everyone, and then one day everyone will just be too scared to pick on each other. That's the plan, and I won't ruin it now. I've already put in far too much time training and planning to let it fall to pieces now.

As I watch them walk down the hall a brilliant idea comes to me that I hadn't thought of before. I almost feel like kicking myself for not thinking of this sooner. It might just fix everything for Colomba. Why don't I transform Colomba into my next soldier? A huge grin spreads across my face at the thought. Colomba would be the perfect soldier; she is a fantastic martial artist so she already knows how to fight, she is willing to work hard to get what she wants, and she is in a lot of pain right now because of these people spreading rumors about her. I can make sure that pain goes away. If she does what I tell her to do I know that she will be happy again. I just know it.

The more I think about it the more I like the idea. It is just perfect. No one will dare to mess with her again. That would certainly make me feel better, knowing that nobody will hurt her again. It would be wonderful to know that I am the reason why she is safe. Nice to know that I'm the reason she's happy again.

As I enter my first period, I try to think about what kind of powers I will give Colomba. I know it has to be something awesome. I wouldn't want to give her some stupid powers that some of the other students would see as pathetic. Maybe I will give her super strength, or maybe something like the ability to control fire. That would be cool. When the teacher starts the class I have a hard time paying attention. I am too busy thinking of superpowers to give to Colomba and how she can get the revenge she deserves for everything that everyone has been saying about her. I will make them regret hurting the only good person in this entire school.

Chapter Three
Colomba-
One of the Few
Friends Left

My first few class periods come and go and before I know it gym has started. As I make my way out of the changing room and into the gym, I walk toward my classmates who have gathered in the center of the basketball court in the middle of the gym. I notice them all move away from me when I get close, giving me dirty looks as they do so. I lower my head as I feel tears threatening to fall down my face.

"Hey there Beautiful. How are you?" Turning around, a smile finally comes over my face as I see Alex coming toward me. Even though most people have stopped talking to me because of these rumors, Alex has stayed by my side. Actually, he has been hanging out with me more since this happened. Either he can see that I am in pain and is trying to support me or he can see that less people are around me and he wants to spend more time with me. I don't know which is his reason, but either way I am happy. With everything that has been happening I have come to rely on Alex more than ever to help me get through the day. He always has a joke to make me laugh or a warm smile to help take away some of the sadness in my heart. I smile at him warmly, happy to finally see a friendly face in this gym.

"I'm doing alright. How are you Alex?" He stands next to me, closer than how friends usually stand next to each other, but I don't move away from him like I used to do. I'm just happy that someone is willingly standing close to me. He has done this to me countless times, but I always moved away before. I always felt uncomfortable to have him so close, but now it feels kind of nice to have him beside me.

"I'm always good when I am around you. You look kinda sad though, you sure you're okay?" When I look at him it doesn't really look like he cares if I am alright or not and is just trying to be polite by asking. I still answer him though, glad to have someone to talk to.

"Yeah I am a bit sad. Everyone is still avoiding me because of those rumors. It's completely nuts that everyone still thinks that I am helping the Crow. I don't know what to do anymore. It all just seems so weird." He shakes his head with a smile on his face.

"People are stupid. They'll come around sooner or later. Don't worry though, you've still got me beside you." If he had said something like that to me a few weeks ago I would have felt uncomfortable by him telling me that I have him, but right now I'm happy that I do. When I look at him I know how much I have come to rely on him recently since he has been one of the only people who has stood beside me. I can't help but think that he seems to be happy that I'm relying on him. It's as if he's happy that this has happened. I push that thought out of my mind as the coach tells us to partner up and shoot some free throws at the basketball hoops. I can't think about my friends like that, especially when I have so few friends with me now. Naturally I partner with Alex to shoot baskets, like I always do in gym. And also, like what always happens, when we play Alex talks the entire time and he only talks about himself.

I listen as he talks about how he has kicked butt in practically every game he has ever played for the basketball and football team. Usually I kind of zone him out whenever he starts going on and on about himself, but today I listen. I pay attention to every word. Since he is one of the only friends I have right now I need to make sure that I try my best to keep him by my side. I don't want to lose what little I have left. When he talks about himself endlessly like this I get super annoyed usually, but now I am eager to listen. I'm not exactly happy to listen, but I just want to listen to let him know how much I value his friendship.

We play and Alex talks for what feels like hours of complete boredom before the coach tells everyone to get ready for our next class. Alex and I part so that we can go into the different locker rooms to get changed and I instantly feel the darkness cloud over me again when he is no longer by my side. All the other girls turn their backs to me whenever I get near them. I get changed as quickly as I can and run out of the room to escape their judging eyes. I don't stop running until I have passed through the gym doors and out into the hallway.

Walking down the hallway with my eyes to the ground, I avoid everyone else's gaze. Alex soon joins me as he walks me to my next class. He walks very close to me, but I let him. Whenever I am around Alex nobody dares to point and whisper about me. I have thought this for a while, but Alex seems to have a power over everyone else in this school. Nobody ever messes with him. Everyone either avoids him or they treat him with a lot of respect, and nothing ever really goes wrong for him. For him, everything just seems so perfect in his life.

I have had this theory for a while that people are afraid of Alex. That's why they treat him so well. They are afraid that if they do anything that he doesn't like then bad things will happen to them. Nobody has ever really said anything bad about him to me, but that's just what I am assuming based on everything that has happened whenever I am around him. People tend to stay away whenever I am near him. They also look away from us, as if they are afraid of making eye contact with him. I only met Alex earlier this year while practically everyone else knew him from middle school. I had gone to a small private school called Doyle Academy while most of the other people in my class went to the public school. Perhaps if I went to the public school instead I may have been able to find out what kind of power he has over everyone. For now though I won't try to think about that. Alex is being kind to me, one of the only people acting kindly to me in this entire school, and I'm not going to try and dig up some dirt on someone who is being kind.

As I look at the people around us avoiding my gaze, I know that I am safe with him. Maybe it is a good thing if I have started hanging out with him more. He has always enjoyed being with me, and I am safe whenever I am with him at school. Maybe being by his side is where I am meant to be. If being beside him means that I am safe from everyone, then I don't want to leave his side.

<u>Chapter Four</u>
Luis-
Colomba as
a Soldier

Almost the entire school day has passed, and I finally have a moment to get out of class to head to the closest empty bathroom. I lock the door behind me and place my hand over the Crow Medal. Almost instantly a large crow appears on the sink counter. The eyes of the crow are full of intelligence and kindness, something most people wouldn't expect to see in the eyes of a bird. Even though birds can't really show emotions with their faces, this bird seems happy to be here. The crow fluffs out its feathers for a moment before it opens its beak to speak to me.

"Hello Master." Shadow greets me with warmth in her voice while I greet her with an excited smile.

"Hi Shadow, I have a wonderful idea that will help someone who really needs it in this school. I just know that this will be the one to end all of the pain in my school forever." Shadows seems to perk up at my words.

"That's wonderful Master. What do you have in mind?"

"I am going to make Colomba my next soldier." Shadow stares at me for a moment in complete silence, as if she is trying to figure out if she heard me correctly, before she speaks again.

"Do you really think that would be the best idea? She has never really been one of your biggest fans. I feel like I need to remind you of that fact since you seem to be forgetting it." Now it is my turn to stare at her in silent disbelief. What is she talking about? This is a great idea, and I know that Colomba will definitely be better because of it. Sometimes Shadow doesn't make any sense. She thinks that she's so smart, but she can be wrong just like everyone else.

"Of course. She will be so much happier once she gives all those people spreading those rumors about her what they deserve. You have heard what people have been saying about her. You can see how much it hurts her. She deserves to get a little revenge on all of them. After all the kind things she has done for people, she doesn't deserve to be treated this way. I will make sure that she is never treated this way again." Shadow flies off of the counter to land on my shoulder. She stares deeply into my eyes, as if she is looking for my soul in there.

"I am not sure that she would feel the same way Master. After all, she might blame you for what happened considering everyone thinks that she is helping you since you were seen carrying her out of that room to safety. Because of that she may not accept the powers you want to give her. She may feel insulted that you are even trying to give her powers." I nod my head, understanding what she means.

"Yeah, but I still want to try. I want to make things better for her. I want her to be happy again." Shadow nods her head.

"Of course. You can try it Master and I hope that things will turn out for the best. I hope that the two of you can both be happy by how this entire situation ends." I smile at her, hoping the same thing.

"Thanks Shadow. Transform me into the Crow, I want to do it now before I lose my nerve." Shadow nods and flies off my shoulder to start flying all around me. She flies faster and faster until I can no longer see her, until she is just a black blur. I blink for a moment and I can tell that I have become the Crow again. Closing my eyes, I make a command even though there is no other person in this room. "Shadow, find Colomba."

I can feel Shadow silently flying through the hallways among the crowds, searching for Colomba. She passes by many classrooms, but she doesn't look in since she can sense that she's not there. Instead, she keeps flying until she finds the girls' bathroom. Flying straight through the closed door, Shadow finds her at the counter, washing her hands. I smile as Shadow enters her heart and I make myself known to her.

<u>Chapter Five</u>
Colomba-
The Voice in
My Head

I scrub my hands at the bathroom sink and I watch as the foamy soap glides off my hands as the water hits it and then rushes down the drain. As I continue to wash my hands a sudden chill comes over me, as if I had dived head first into a pool of ice water. Did someone open a window or something? Why is it so cold in here? A shiver runs through my body as a horrific voice seems to echo in my mind.

Hello Colomba. I practically leap around to see the room behind me, yet there is nobody there. No, no, no, please let this be some kind of prank. My heart pounds in my chest as I stare at the room around me. Hoping to find someone hiding somewhere. Hoping that the voice doesn't belong to who I think it does. You don't have to be afraid Colomba. I am the Crow. Dang it, that is what I was afraid of!

"What do you want from me?" Does he know who I really am? Is that why he is contacting me through my mind? I am more afraid than I have ever been in my entire life. My eyes constantly scan the room, expecting the Crow to pop out at any minute with some of his shadow dogs so that he can rip me apart. That is what he wants isn't it? To take me down so that he can take over the school and make everyone suffer because some people here decide to pick on each other. What am I going to do now that he knows who I am?

I want to help you Colomba, I swear it. I have heard what people have been saying about you, cruel words, words that are not true. I can give you the power you need to make sure that nobody will ever hurt you with their words again. You will be safe. I can make sure that you will be safe.

Looking at myself in the mirror, I almost scream at what I see. My eyes are not their usual aquamarine blue, now they are solid black. I can't even see the whites of my eyes. They too have been consumed by the darkness. I almost look as if I have been possessed by a demon or something. I guess, in a way, I have. When I see the blackness in my eyes I feel rage build up inside of me and I say something that I know I will regret later.

"I would rather die than be controlled by you. Go find somebody else to lie to because I won't listen." Silence follows my words and I automatically realize that I have just made my arch nemesis super mad. Well… I'm going to die. I am going to die today. It has been a short life, but a good one. The Crow is going to kill me I just know it. Well at least I died doing what is right, telling the Crow that I won't fall into his trap to hurt other people.

I don't want to control you Colomba. He almost sounds as if I have hurt his feelings. The Crow doesn't sound mad at all, he sounds… sad. What on earth am I hearing? I never expected someone like the Crow to be so sensitive about one insult. I almost want to apologize to him. It's just something I naturally do whenever I feel as if I have hurt someone, I want to apologize, but I am definitely not doing that now. After everything this guy has done he doesn't deserve an apology from me. He deserved to hear what I just said. I want to help you. I am the only one who can protect you from all of those terrible people around you. You have got to be kidding me. This guy thinks that he can help me? Oh please. If he makes me one of his little slaves then nobody will ever trust me again. They will think that they have proof that I am helping the Crow.

"No, you are the one who got me into this mess in the first place. Everyone thinks that I am siding with you because you carried me out of that classroom when my leg was trapped. You could have just left me in that classroom and none of this would have happened. I would have been fine, but you let the whole world see you helping me and now everything is terrible. I am grateful that you helped me by getting those rocks off, but you didn't have to do anything more than that. I would have been fine if you left me there, but you had to let everyone see you carrying me and make them think that I'm helping you!" Once again the two of us are stuck in silence and I silently pray that he won't kill me for saying such mean words.

I was not responsible for that! If you want someone to blame look at all of the people around you! They were the ones who turned their backs on you! I didn't do that though. I helped you then and I will help you now. Unlike them, I have your back. I want to help you be happy again.

"They turned their backs on me because they think I am helping you! They think that I am the enemy! If I was in their shoes I would be a bit afraid to be near me too! It's understandable, it doesn't feel good to live through, but it's understandable! You, on the other hand, are not understandable. You are trying to give me power so that I can hurt people. That isn't understandable at all, it's absolutely crazy! You're crazy if you think that I will ever help you after everything you have done to the people in this town! You have filled everyone with fear, but I am not afraid of you! I can only feel anger toward you!" The silence has returned and it hangs between the two of us. My heart races rapidly in my chest as I wait for his anger to spill over and for him to take it out on me, but nothing happens. Finally he breaks the silence with a dark tone in his voice.

I see... Well if you change your mind Colomba, I will be there to help you. No matter what you may think, I am here to help those who are in pain. All of a sudden, the cold feeling that had been surrounding me vanishes and I somehow know that the Crow has left me. Turning around, I look into my reflection in the bathroom mirror and smile when I see that my eyes are no longer a terrifying black, but back to their normal cheerful bright blue. I sigh in relief when I see that they are back to normal, but that relief only lasts for a moment.

I can't believe that the Crow tried to possess me! Out of everyone in this school he chose me! Kind of ironic that he tried to choose me when I am actually the enemy who has defeated him several times. I almost want to laugh at that irony, but then I really think about what just happened and I am overcome by fear again. The Crow could sense that I am weakening because of everything that people have been saying about me. He thinks that I will fall prey to him just because of that? Well then he has another surprise waiting for him. No matter what happens to me I will never even think about joining his side.

Quickly drying off my hands I march out the door and through the halls to get back to class. I am overcome with anger at the Crow for even thinking about making me one of his slaves. I am angry at myself too for being in such a position that the Crow thinks that he can "help me". I feel pretty pathetic right now.

I make it to my class and sit down at my desk so that I can continue reading a book from the library. All around me the room is silent, but I can't help but keep thinking about what was said in the bathroom. I blamed him for what happened and he denied it. How could he deny it? Everything that has happened was because of what he did, so how could he deny it? Is this guy really so blind that he can't even tell when something is his fault?

My mind is too filled with angry thoughts to even focus on my book. I put the book back into my bag and set my head on the table. It feels nice to have the cool surface of the desk against my cheek, especially after being so angry. Whenever I get angry I feel warm all over. To help calm myself down when I start feeling angry, I usually find a way to cool myself off. After everything that has been going on recently I have found that I am doing this more and more often. With my head still resting on my desk, I look around the classroom, feeling everyone's hatred of me crushing me like a bug. I look away from them all, to avoid their condemning eyes, but I can still feel their loathing directed at me, making me want to hide. In this school though, there is no place that I can really hide.

Chapter Six
Luis-
Rosie

I lean against the bathroom sink counter and bury my face in my hands, trying to understand what just happened. Colomba just turned me down? Why did she turn me down? I was giving her everything that she needed, but she said no and yelled at me like I'm the villain here! She told me that all of this is my fault even though I'm the one that helped her! I don't understand this at all.

Lifting my head from my hands, I can see that Shadow is perched on the counter beside me staring at me intently.

"Say out loud what is bothering you Master. It will be better for you if you express it." I sigh, knowing that she is right, like usual.

"I don't understand. Why would she give up something like this? Why would she give up having superpowers and getting the revenge she deserves?" Shadow looks away from me, staring off into the distance. This is something she does whenever she's about to say something important.

"Maybe it is simply not what she wishes to do. Maybe she doesn't want to take her anger out on others. Maybe she doesn't want revenge." I look away from her, feeling a little guilty as I respond to her with my honest answer.

"I would have done it. Why wouldn't she?" I feel something land on my shoulder. Glancing over, I see that it is Shadow. She pushes my bangs out of my eyes with her beak, something she always does when she is trying to comfort me.

"Perhaps because she is not you." I look away from her, knowing that she is making a valid point. Colomba isn't me, she isn't even remotely like me. I'm pretty much a pathetic loser while she is all around amazing; she's smart, she's athletic, she's kind, and she's beautiful. I have always known that she isn't like me. I guess what just happened proved me right.

"I guess you're right Shadow. I should probably get back to class before the teacher starts getting curious about where I am." I place my hand on the medal and she immediately disappears as if she wasn't even here. I honestly don't think the teacher would notice, or care, if I went back to class at all. I just didn't want to hear any more about what Shadow has to say about what just happened. I want to be alone right now. I leave the bathroom and walk down the hall back to class.

Since no one else is in the hallway, my footfalls echo and thunder with every step. I can't believe what just happened. I never expected Colomba to turn me down. After everything she has gone through recently I would have bet anything that she would have said yes to the power I could have given her. I wish I could just give her the powers anyway, but I can only give people these powers if they accept them willingly. I can't force them to have this power. More than anything I want to give her these powers so that everyone will stop hurting her. I want her to be happy again. I want to see her smile again. It feels like so long since I have seen a true smile on her face. One of the things that I love about her the most is the brightness in her eyes, eyes full of life, but with everything that has been going on with her that light is dimming.

Why did she have to say no? Why couldn't she just take these powers when she was given the chance? I know that she's mad at me since everyone thinks that she is siding with me, but couldn't she just accept the help I was trying to give to her? I mean, it's not like I did anything wrong.

Turning around a corner, I run straight into someone who has their head down. Looking down, I see a very skinny girl with long, straight blonde hair that falls in her face. Her skin is tanned, and dirt is present under her fingernails. I recognize this girl from back in middle school. We never really talked, but everyone knows who she is because of what everyone has labeled her. It is hard for someone with her label to not be known wherever they are. I have a label myself as the school loser, but they do not compare to the things that I have heard people call her.

"Hi Rosie, how are you?" Rosie doesn't look into my eyes when I speak to her, but I don't expect her to. She never does with anybody. She doesn't look in my eyes, not because she is shy, but for another reason.

"Fine." She walks away without another word, not really realizing that she is being rude by not asking me how I am doing or at least saying goodbye first. I watch her for a moment as she goes back to class. As I watch her walk farther and farther from me, I feel a sense of pity come over me.

Rosie is someone that doesn't really speak to anybody, mainly because she is not really interested in the company of others unless they can talk to her about very specific things. Her family owns the greenhouses in town where everyone buys their houseplants. Rosie can tell you everything about any plant or flower that you can think of without a moment of thought. Her knowledge on that subject is amazing, beyond the ability of practically anybody else, but her skills with people are definitely not at the same level. Rosie is seen as awkward by most people until they find out the real reason for why she acts the way she does.

Just like everyone else in this school, Rosie has a label, but hers is a lot more isolating and painful. To those who are kinder they call her special or mentally disabled, but I have heard many other people call her names that are far less kind.

I turn away from Rosie's retreating figure as I head to my own class. I am left alone with thoughts of Colomba and Rosie, wondering how I could help both of them, possibly at the same time.

Chapter Seven
Colomba-
The Flower Girl

Walking through the halls on my own, a new school day has started and I already want to go home. Just like every day the past few weeks, people are staring at me, saying things about me when they think I can't hear them, and insulting me as if it's nothing. My head hangs low as I try to be as invisible as possible to everyone around me, but it doesn't work.

My mind keeps flashing back to what happened yesterday when the Crow crept into my mind and tried to turn me over to his side, to make me one of his little cronies. I completely hate my life right now. Why on earth would he think that I would ever help him? Everyone hates me because of him. His logic is messed up. Maybe he did all of that on purpose. Maybe he let everyone see him rescue me so that everyone would abandon me and then I would be weak and then I would be easier to convince to join his side because I would want to get revenge on all of these people who have been so hurtful to me... Okay, probably not. I am giving him way too much credit. I mean he is the guy who thinks that he can give bullied kids superpowers so that they can get revenge and he thinks that everything is going to turn out alright with all that in the end. I'm not really dealing with someone who is super smart. A guy like the Crow can't come up with a super sophisticated plan like that. What was I thinking with that anyway? I must be getting really messed up in the head to be thinking stuff like that. I really need to just relax. I force those thoughts out of my head as I continue walking down the hall.

Even though I am sending off vibes stating that I don't want to be bothered with my lowered head and the fact that I'm not looking at anybody, someone doesn't understand the hint I am giving and does something completely unexpected. One second I am looking at the dirty floor of my school hallway and the next I am looking straight into the petals of a bright pink flower. Leaping backward I look up to see a girl with long blonde hair and tanned skin. Even though she nearly shoved a flower up my nose, she isn't looking me in the eyes as she speaks to me.

"Hi, my name is Rosie. My family owns the Penderson Greenhouses. This flower was grown in that greenhouse and we would like for you to have it as a gift from us to you." She states this as if she is reading from a script that someone had prepared for her, but she is bored and isn't interested in reading it at all. My mind suddenly flashes through some of my memories and I remember who this girl is. I have never actually met her, but I have heard of her.

My grandmother and I frequently go to her family's greenhouse to get flowers and other plants for our garden. Her parents are both very sweet and gentle people that my grandma and I love talking to. They love talking about their daughter, who they absolutely adore, but who also has a problem. She is autistic and has a lot of issues making friends and getting picked on. It has been like this since she was a little girl. Her form of autism is called Aspergers. Most people who are autistic are usually put in, what a lot of people call "the special classes" at my school, but since Rosie is considered "high functioning", or able to function pretty normally, she is in the regular classes with everyone else.

I take the flower from her, giving her a smile that she only sees when she glances up at me for a moment, never letting her eyes remain on my face for more than a second.

"Thank you Rosie, my grandma and I go to your family's greenhouses a lot to get plants. Are your parents having you pass out flowers to advertise?"

"Yeah, they also said that it will help me talk to people more." Most people wouldn't have said that since it would be awkward, but Rosie doesn't really seem to care.

"Well I'm sure it will work out well. Your parents have told me that you really like flowers, can you tell me about this one?" I already know what it is, it's a carnation, but if her parents want to use this opportunity to have Rosie talk to more people then I'll try to help out. Besides I think Rosie and I could be really good friends. I have always enjoyed gardening and from what her parents have said, plants are all that Rosie really cares about in the world.

Rosie perks up when I ask her about the flower and her blue eyes light up in excitement.

"That is a dianthus caryophyllus, clove pink, or the carnation. It is a species of dianthus and is thought to be originally from the Mediterranean region, but that is currently unknown. This flower was used in ceremonial crowns in Greece a long time ago. Medically it is used to treat upset stomachs and to help with fevers. It also…" She stops suddenly as if she has just figured out something important. "I've talked too much haven't I? My parents say that I talk a lot when I talk about plants and it might make people uncomfortable or bored." I smile at her, trying to make her feel better.

"It's alright, it's very fascinating and I do love flowers as well." The warning bell rings and Rosie gives me a quick, "Bye" before she runs off to her next class, leaving me alone with my little flower.

As I walk to my next class I stare down at the pretty little pink flower, finding a bit of joy holding something so beautiful. When I am going through the doorway to my classroom, a familiar feeling comes over me. The feeling that something bad is about to happen. I glance back to see Rosie down the hall trying to give someone else a flower. My entire body tenses in anticipation when I see who it is, Angela. Rosie tries to give Angela a beautiful little daisy, but Angela just sneers at the kind gift as if Rosie is handing her a creepy bug or something.

"I don't want your smelly weed you idiot. Why would I ever want something from someone like you?" Angela marches away from her while Rosie holds the flower closely to herself, as if she is trying to comfort the little daisy. Before I can walk over there to comfort her, Rosie walks away with tears beginning to fall down her face. I walk back into my classroom feeling defeated. I have to be the worst superhero ever. Not only did my arch nemesis (or whatever he is, I don't really know) try and make me one of his little slaves, but I couldn't even save one person from being hurt by someone else. Not only that, but the whole school thinks I'm on the bad guy's side too because of what happened when the Sprinter attacked the school. I am so pathetic.

I walk into the classroom, fighting every urge to just walk out and go into the bathroom so I could have the privacy necessary to cry my eyes out. To think that a few weeks ago I loved coming to school every day, now I dread every second. It is kind of depressing to think about. Now I feel completely lost and there is nobody here to help save me.

Chapter Eight
Luis-
The Rumors

The ticking of the clock on the wall seems to echo in the silent room as everyone else finishes up their quizzes. I finished mine a few minutes ago, along with a few other people in the front of the class where I am sitting. So now I am sitting quietly thinking to myself.

My thoughts keep going back to what Colomba had said to me when I had tried to give her superpowers so that she can get her revenge. She told me that it's my fault that she is in this position. I'm the reason she is getting hurt. I can't believe that she said that to me! I mean, I'm the one who saved her from having her leg crushed when the Sprinter was running around the school. I saved her; I didn't hurt her! It's all these stupid people in the school, it's their fault. They saw me helping her and now they won't leave her alone. It's their fault, not mine. All of the people in this school are idiots for believing every rumor they hear, just like how they have always believed what everyone says about me.

As these dark thoughts seem to circle around my head, someone else's voice invades my mind.

"I heard that she is working with the Crow, Colomba acts as his spy inside the school and then she tells the Crow who to take over and what powers to give them." I turn my head slightly to look over at two of my classmates sitting beside me, leaning in close so that they can whisper to each other.

"I always thought that the Crow wouldn't need anybody like that in the school since he is probably a student here. I mean he always knows what is going on here and can somehow get inside the school to affect everyone that he gives powers to. That must mean that he goes to school with us, right?" The person who had spoken first shakes his head.

"I doubt that. I bet he's an adult. I think that because he probably invented some kind of machine or something that gives him those powers. I bet those wings on his back are just some kind of machine and those dog things he creates are like nanobots or something. The powers he gives everyone probably come from a secret potion or something. I bet he's a scientist, that's why he was able to create all of this stuff." I have to cover my mouth to keep myself from laughing. Wow this guy is dumb. That isn't even close to how I got my powers or who I really am. I wonder what he would say if he found out that the person he is so afraid of is only three feet away from him. I bet he would pee his pants in fear. That thought actually makes me smile and I have to hold back a laugh again.

"Well, I guess that makes sense." Judging from the way he said that, I'm guessing this guy agrees with everything his friend says, no matter what it may be. I would pity him if he wasn't agreeing with this guy about a lie he's telling about Colomba and me.

"Trust me, if you want to stay safe in this school, stay away from Colomba or else you might get possessed by the Crow next." I want to go over there and give that guy a piece of my mind, but I know that would only get me in trouble for yelling at someone during a quiz.

Are these the kinds of rumors that have been spreading about Colomba all this time? Barely anyone even talks to me, so I don't really hear a lot of gossip, but I have overheard a few things being said about her. I never thought it would be so bad that it would spread to a bunch of people who obviously don't even know Colomba. Anybody who knows her would know that she is too nice to want to harm anyone, which is what they think she is doing if she is on my side as the Crow. They think that she is a monster.

While I sit there, wanting to say something to them, they keep talking about her as if she is the worst human being to ever set foot on this planet. It feels as if my anger will boil over at any second and I will just explode. What is wrong with these people? Can't they see that what they are saying are complete lies? Why is everyone so blind to the truth? Why am I the only one that sees the truth? Why can't they see that neither Colomba nor I am the villain here? We are just two people trying to survive, and I am trying to make sure that nobody gets hurt ever again. I think back on what Colomba had told me when I had tried to give her superpowers. She thinks that I am the bad guy too, and that I am the reason she is being hurt now.

As I listen to them go on and on about her I can't help but wonder, was Colomba right? Is it really my fault that she is being hurt? Am I responsible for all of this?... No! It is not my fault! It never was and it never will be! I did not want anything bad to happen! I was helping her! I will never hurt her. I will never hurt anybody the way that everybody else has always hurt me. I don't want to hurt anybody.

The class period passes by quickly for me and I rush out the door so that I won't be tempted to say something cruel to those two idiots. I pass by countless people in the hall as they bump and push into each other in the crowded space. None of them say excuse me or apologize, they don't care at all. Many people bump into me, most don't even look at me as they do it while some look back at me with amusement, as if they planned on bumping into me like that. With all of the stuff that people do to me, I wouldn't be surprised if they did bump into me on purpose. A lot of people here like doing little things like that to me throughout the day. Apparently, harassing someone else helps break up the boring routine of the day. I wish they had just remained bored.

Turning down another hallway I see that one girl that I had talked to the other day, Rosie. I have heard people talking about how she had been passing out flowers the other day to help advertise for her parents' greenhouse and to help her talk to more people, but the school had to call her parents because some kids had been teasing her about it. I haven't heard anything about any of the kids who made fun of her getting in trouble for it, but I kind of doubt that they did. Nobody ever gets in trouble when they deserve it around here. Since she no longer has any flowers with her. I'm guessing that her parents have given up on that idea to help her socialize.

She is pulling a few things out of her locker before slamming it closed and turning around to walk straight into a guy who drops all of his books to the floor. The guy glares at her for her honest mistake. It was obvious that she just didn't see him, but that doesn't matter to him, he just wants to let his anger out on her.

"Nice going genius, aren't you graceful. I bet you get that all the time Rosie." The guy states this sarcastically but Rosie smiles softly, blushing a little as if she is happy about his remark.

"Thank you." She practically whispers this to him before walking away with an honest smile on her face. Both me, and the guy who had insulted her, stare at her completely confused as she continues on her way down the hallway. It takes me a moment to figure out what just happened. Rosie didn't understand what just happened. I don't know too much about people who have autism, but I do know one thing, they don't understand sarcasm or a lot of jokes very well. People who are autistic usually take things very literally, which makes things a whole lot more difficult for them when talking to people who don't have autism. That's what happened here with that guy. He had said something sarcastic, but she didn't realize it and so she thought that he was being serious. She thought that when he called her a genius that he meant it. That's why she looked so happy about what he said and thanked him.

As I watch this guy pick up his books scattered across the floor I wonder something to myself. If a person doesn't realize that they are getting made fun of does it count as bullying? I mean Rosie didn't seem hurt at all when he said that to her, and part of the whole bullying thing is that someone has to be hurt or insulted. Rosie was neither, so what is this? Is this bullying, or is this someone being mean for no reason since the person they're talking to doesn't get it? When I look into the anger filled gaze of the guy who had insulted Rosie as he glares at her retreating figure down the hall, I think I know my answer. No matter if she understood or not this is still bullying. The ones who hurt and insult people that don't understand are still guilty just like the rest of them in this school. Almost every single person in this school is guilty of the same crime. They all hurt those who are different than them and they don't deserve any mercy when I become the Crow. They don't deserve mercy, and they won't get any. Not from me.

I start walking back to class again, not stopping to help the mean guy who had teased Rosie pick up his books. He doesn't deserve my help. My hands are clenched into fists at my side as I pass through the halls, looking at all the other people around me. They all laugh and talk with each other while I am in solitary silence. They are all happy and enjoying the company of the people around them, and I hate them for it. They get to be with the people they care about while I am stuck alone.

I want to be able to walk down the halls again with Colomba and Nat without worrying about Alex doing anything to me or to all of us for what I did to him. I want to be able to just be happy again instead of having to worry about what will happen. I am always afraid, thinking that Alex is going to jump out from around the corner or sneak up behind me. I feel like a paranoid, crazy person.

Once, in fifth grade, I had talked to a girl that Alex had liked and I had to suffer because of that too. Apparently asking a girl if you could borrow a pencil is a terrible thing to do in Alex's book. During recess I had gone inside to go to the bathroom. What I didn't know then was that Alex and a few of his friends were following me there. I wasn't as observant then as I am now.

As soon as we were all in the bathroom, all three of them grabbed me and dragged in one of the stalls while I kicked and tried to run away, begging them to let me go, telling them that I didn't do anything. Of course, they didn't listen to me. They took me into one of the stalls and forced me to kneel in front of the toilet. I kept begging them to stop, but that only made what happened even worse. Since my mouth was open to beg, when they grabbed the back of my head and forced my head into the toilet I got a mouth full of toilet water. When my head was under I could feel the air bubbles escaping from my mouth and swarming across my face to pop on the surface. Alex and his two friends must have been making a ton of noise since I could hear them laughing even though my head was completely under water. It sounded muffled and unclear, but I could still tell it was laughter. I have had plenty of experience with people laughing at me so I know when they are doing it.

They grabbed a handful of my hair and lifted my head up so that I could take in a massive lung full of air. They didn't show me mercy though. As soon as I took a few breaths I was back under the water. I tried to move my arms backward to try and hit them, to try and get their hands off of me, but they just grabbed my hands and held on to me so that I couldn't move. They dunked me about three or four more times before they finally left me alone. All of them were laughing as they walked out the bathroom, leaving me soaking wet and completely humiliated.

I got up off the floor and walked over to the mirror over the sinks and saw me as I really was, as I really am, a complete loser. In my reflection I watched the water drip down from my hair and fall down into the sink in an endless stream. The top half of my shirt was wet from my dripping hair and when the water splashed when I was trying to get away. The smell radiating off of me was terrible. I smelled like a men's room in a rundown gas station. For those of you who have never been in one, it's not pleasant. I looked so pathetic that day, my entire body seemed to sag like a flower that had recently been rained on. The person in the mirror was someone who had been completely defeated, one who had no hope left in them.

What really caught my eye though about the image in the mirror were the eyes of the person staring back at me. In those eyes defeat was not there, only deep rage. A fire seemed to burn in those eyes, a fire created from hate. Even though the body was defeated, the soul still wanted to fight. At that moment, I wanted to run out the bathroom door and catch up with Alex. I wanted to beat him senseless and then drag him into one of the bathroom stalls so that I could dunk his head in the toilet. I wanted to make him feel every single terrible thing he ever did to me. I wanted to show no mercy.

I may have gotten the Crow Medal years later, but I think that that is the day that I truly became the Crow. Before that day I still had some hope that things could get better. After almost getting drowned in a toilet for a stupid reason like talking to a girl, you kind of lose hope in just about everything. After that day I just lived each day, just trying to survive but not expecting anything good to ever happen. That all changed though when this year started. On the first day of school the unexpected happened, and I'm not talking about getting a magical medal that gives me superpowers. That day I had someone stick up for me and helped me. I had someone become my friend that day. Colomba did that for me and now I am abandoning her when she really needs a friend because I want to protect her from whatever Alex now has planned for me.

Why can't this all end? Why can't I just be happy? What did I do to any of these people that makes them think that it's alright to hurt me? Why am I the one they chose to do all these terrible things to?

I overhear what they say about me as the Crow. They think that I am a monster for everything that I have done. I almost want to laugh out loud when I think that as I finally make it to my classroom. If I am the monster then you are the ones that made me that way.

<u>Chapter Nine</u>
Colomba-
The Pain
I Feel

Making my way through the halls feels like I am walking to my doom. All around me people are staring at me, and they aren't even trying to hide it. It feels as if I am some kind of attraction at a zoo or something, just there for people to stare at and whisper about. Just like the animals in the zoo, when the people whisper and point at me, I can't do a thing about it. I can only keep walking and hope that one day they will stop.

I weave through the roaring crowd around me to head to class. The usual noise of the hallway seems to beat against me as I remain in silence with no one to talk to. Trying to make my way through the endless crowd of people, someone makes a move against me that I don't notice until it is too late. From the corner of my eye I see something shoot out in front of me, but it is too fast, I don't have time to react to protect myself. A person's foot cuts in front of me and I trip over it; my books fly out of my hands and scatter over the floor. While I quickly try to pick them up the entire world seems to fall silent before everyone laughs at me. As I kneel in the middle of the hallway, trying to gather my books, everyone laughs and nobody helps me. Why are they laughing? Can't they see that I'm upset? Can't they see that I'm in pain watching them laugh at me like this? Don't they know how much it hurts to be laughed at? Why are they being so cruel to me when I have done nothing to them? Why are they laughing at my pain?

When I have gathered all of my books I run through the crowd that is still laughing behind me. They laugh at the person they think of as a traitor, because they think I helped the Crow, someone I would rather die than help in his miserable little crusade.

I make it to my desk in my next class, practically breathless since I ran the entire way, hoping that could prevent anyone from doing anything else to me. There are still a few minutes left before class begins so I open a book and pretend to read it, hoping that this will stop anyone from trying to talk to me. That doesn't work though, lucky me (Ps, that was sarcasm).

A boy walks over and stands in front of my desk with a friendly smile on his face. The first friendly smile I've seen in a long time. Even though it is a friendly smile I feel a bit nervous when I see who the smile belongs to. I know who this boy is, but I have never actually met him. His name is Joel, and he is one of the many kids in this school who is picked on constantly. Apparently, everyone used to pick on him because he is a bit of a computer nerd. Now everyone makes fun of him for a different reason. I have heard that Joel is the leader of the Crow's fan club. Naturally, the school didn't let them form an official club so they have a secret one that meets after school once a week at a diner down the street from the school. It is a club made up of many of the bullied kids in my school, a club that wants to see my downfall as Silver Dove. As I look up at Joel now, a sickening feeling invades my stomach and I want to puke.

"Hey Colomba." I try to return his smile, but I can tell that it's weak. It's hard to be friendly to the guy who leads a club that wants you to fail.

"Hi Joel, what's up?" He leans in close to me as if he is about to say something top secret, as if we are best buds.

"I'm guessing you know that I lead the Crow's fan club around here," No duh, everybody knows that. I would have to be an idiot not to know that. "We would love it if you could join us." I feel my hands tighten into fists underneath my desk.

"What?" That single word comes out as a soft, growling whisper as I try to bury my anger.

"Well, since you are helping the Crow, we would like to help you guys in any way we can. If you join us we can stay in contact and do whatever he needs us to do. We can be his army in this school. With all of our help I'm sure that we can win." My eyes grow wide and my fists are so tight that I can feel my fingernails digging into my palms. This guy thinks that I am helping the Crow too? He wants me to join his group to defeat Silver

Dove, AKA *me*? He even wants his club to be the Crow's army; what on earth is wrong with him? Why would he and all of his followers willingly become an "army" to fight everyone else at this school and join sides with someone who only causes mayhem and possesses people? I swallow back my anger as I reply to him.

"I'm not the Crow's helper Joel and I never will be. Despite what everyone says, I don't even support what the Crow is doing. I don't want to join your group. Thank you for asking though." Joel smiles at me as he shakes his head.

"You don't have to pretend with me Colomba, we're on the same side. My friends and I can help you. You don't have to be afraid all the time if you have us to help watch your back. We can help protect each other. We will watch over you at school and make sure you're never alone, and you can tell the Crow to help us." It takes everything I have to not yell at him. Instead I somehow maintain my polite tone.

"I am not pretending Joel, and I do not need your help. I am fine." The teacher walks into the room and class begins. Joel walks away from me looking very confused, but I won't bother trying to explain things to him again. It's not worth it. He will be just like the rest, no matter how many times I will try to explain myself to him he won't believe me. Nobody ever believes me now.

When I have finished the assignment that the teacher gives us I ask the teacher if I can go to the bathroom. I wander slowly down the hall, wanting the time to pass by so that I won't have to spend any more time in that classroom, listening to people whispering about me since they think I can't hear them. As I pass by one classroom I pause for a moment when I see a familiar face through the open doorway. Inside the room, the class is silently working on an assignment, but Rosie, who is sitting in the front row near the door, already seems to have finished since she is preoccupied with something else.

On her desk she has three pencil in a perfect line across her desk. It almost looks as if she used a ruler to make them that straight. Each pencil is lined up from tip to eraser, each pencil perfectly sharpened. I have heard that people who are autistic tend to have unusual habits or quirks that most people don't understand. Many of these habits usually involve placing things in a specific order that they have set up in their heads. Why do they have these desires to place things in a certain order? I have absolutely no idea, but I don't mind it at all. It doesn't affect me, or bother me, in any way so why should I concern myself about it? Apparently, the boy sitting next to Rosie doesn't share my opinion about this though.

Every time that Rosie has her eyes turned away from her pencils the boy sitting next to her leans across toward her so that he can knock one of the pencils off the desk and quickly go back to his seat so that Rosie can go through the process of straightening out the pencils so that he can do it all over again. Several other people around them are chuckling at this cruel display and none of them even look like they want to help Rosie at all. It's as if they are watching a side show at a carnival, and she is the clown. This clown isn't smiling though. As this keeps repeating, I see tears forming in her eyes that she is fighting to keep back.

I watch in revulsion as this is repeated four times while everyone just watches and laughs. I want to run in there and give that guy knocking the pencils off her desk a piece of my mind. I want to tell the teacher, as well as the entire class, that they should be ashamed for letting this go on, but I know I can't do that. I can't just walk in some random classroom and start yelling at people. Due to everything that has been happening to me nobody would listen to what I have to say about how they're treating Rosie. In fact I might actually make things worse for her. If an outcast like me starts defending her then she will look even more like a loser in their eyes. Plus everyone already thinks that I am helping the Crow, if I start yelling at people about bullying each other then it will only make things worse. I don't know how things can get worse for me, but I'm sure the universe isn't done with punishing me yet for something I didn't do. I know that the universe has just been enjoying making me miserable recently so I'm sure it could come up with something.

I hurry down the hall and make it to the bathroom, but I only wanted to come in here so that I could be alone. A few weeks ago I loved the company of other people, now more than anything I want to be alone most of the time. I know that if I'm around other people they might turn on me, they might hurt me. I look at myself in the bathroom mirror and see a set of miserable blue eyes staring right back at me. There is no hope in those eyes, only deep pain.

I feel so weak. How can someone who has superpowers, and has vowed to help make everyone's lives better in this school, have just completely turned their back on someone as defenseless as Rosie? I could have walked in there, it may have ended badly, but shouldn't I have taken the risk? Isn't that what heroes are supposed to do, take risks to help people? Why didn't I do it? Why didn't I help her? I think I know the answer to that question though, and I don't like it. After everything that has happened to me I am afraid to stand up against these people. I don't want people to pick on me more than they do now so I stayed quiet even when I should have said something. I am such a pathetic loser.

I think back to how the Crow had tried to give me powers to fight back against everyone who is hurting me. I can't fight them as Silver Dove since everyone views her as a hero, but as some other person with superpowers things would be different. I could have taken them down with those powers and nobody would think badly about Silver Dove, I would be safe. Maybe I should have… *No!* No, I can't think like that! Yes, yes all of this has been awful to live through, but getting revenge isn't the option. I have already told that to several other people who have gotten powers from the Crow, now I just need to follow my own advice. I need to learn how to live with this. I need to find a way to conquer this before I completely lose hope. This may be bad, but it won't last forever. At least I hope it doesn't. I don't know what I would do if all of this never stops.

<u>Chapter Ten</u>
Luis-
The Unexpected
Meeting

The art room is buzzing with activity while everyone starts working on their new assignments that Mr. Sizemore just gave to us. He has already had us draw birds and trees as an assignment, and now for this week our assignment is to draw any animal we please. Since we have the choice, everyone is drawing an animal they love. That is everyone except me. I am drawing an animal I hate. Ever since I was a little kid I have been absolutely terrified of dogs. One day, when I was walking home from a store where I had been buying some candy, a stray dog started chasing me and bit me on the leg. Ever since then I have been afraid of dogs. I still have a scar on my leg from that terrible day. I actually had to go to the hospital to get stitches for it. A very scary experience for a six-year-old kid.

Even though I don't really like dogs, I am still drawing one because of what this particular dog means to me. I will never admit this to anyone, but the dog I am drawing right now is one of my demon dogs, the shadow like monsters I create when I become the Crow. It is a huge black dog with its lips pulled up in a ferocious snarl. Its pointed ears almost look like demon horns. Its menacing eyes glare at whoever looks at the picture with pure hatred. The monstrous dog has turned out better than I expected it to. I almost shiver in fear just looking at the picture. I made sure that I put this drawing in my special sketchbook. This sketchbook is the one that I consider to be my record as the Crow. I have drawings of myself as the Crow, all of the people I have transformed, and now a picture of one of my shadow dogs.

Closing my sketchbook on my finished picture, I look around at the other people in the classroom. They are all busy talking with each other while they work on their sketches, none of them even think about talking to me. I am all alone here. Despite the fact that I am alone I still consider this one of my favorite classes. Art is something that I have always loved. Whenever I would be upset from someone picking on me, I would pick up a pencil and start sketching something until I felt at least a little bit better. Drawing is something that is almost healing for me. It may not make all of the bad things that happen to me disappear, but it helps me feel better after they happen. What also makes this class fantastic is the teacher, Mr. Sizemore. Mr. Sizemore is the kind of teacher that you know really cares about each and every one of his students. He has a cool, calm, and collected attitude that automatically makes you comfortable around him.

He's someone you know that you can trust. In class he always has positive encouragement ready to give to a struggling student and a helping hand to whoever needs it.

Across the room, Alex is showing off his sketch of a grizzly bear (a really bad sketch). I'm not surprised that a guy like him would draw something as big and stupid as a bear. He and the bear almost match; both of them are big, muscular, and dumb as a rock. Rage rises in me as I watch him show off to his friends with a huge grin on his face. It's all because of him that I feel so miserable right now. I have to avoid the people I have become friends with, Colomba and Nat, because I know that Alex is planning on getting revenge on me and if they get involved then they will get hurt too. I couldn't live with myself if Alex hurt them, especially if he hurt Colomba.

A thought races through my mind that has honestly passed through my mind many times; what would it be like if I could switch places with Alex?

First off, I know what I wouldn't do. I wouldn't tease everyone the way he has always done. I would be kinder than he ever was, except to one person. I would be just as cruel to him as he is to me. I would make him regret every insult he said to me, every time he hit me, every time he made me want to just give up on everything. I could walk down the halls without fear of anybody hurting me or trying to trip me. I could talk freely and not be afraid that somebody will put me down for something I said or just tell me to shut up. And I could actually have friends who won't be afraid to hang out with me in case they get made fun of too for associating with me.

I smile when I think of one other possibility. I could finally ask Colomba out without any fear of being hurt by someone or having her being hurt. I know that if I were to ask her out now then she would probably say no. I mean, who would want to go out with a pathetic guy like me who gets picked on all the time? Even if she did say yes, then everyone would tease her for going out with a weirdo like me. For some reason she doesn't see me as a weirdo right now like everyone else, but if they started making fun of her for it she might start joining their side. Alex would be upset with her if she said yes as well since he has a crush on her too and he would make her miserable for choosing me instead of him. I've known him long enough to know that that is exactly what he would do if that happened. That's why I have to change things at this school before I even dare to try and ask her out, or to even really do anything.

As these dark thoughts rush through my head the bell rings, signaling the end of class. I quickly grab my things and run out the door, making sure that Alex won't be able to keep up with me so that he could try something. More than anything I hope that he will just forget about how I tripped him into that puddle a few weeks ago and will just leave me alone, but I won't hold my breath.

Rushing through the halls, when I am about to turn a corner, I almost run smack into someone I had hoped I wouldn't be close to for quite a while, Colomba. Her eyes grow wide when she sees that we almost collided, but her surprise quickly melts into a smile when she sees *who* she almost walked into.

"Oh Luis, I'm so sorry. I didn't mean to almost run into you like that." I lower my gaze from hers, not wanting her to see how happy I am to be talking to her again. I am so stupid. How could I let this happen? I should have just run before she had a chance to see who she had almost bumped into.

"It- it's alright Colomba, no big deal."

"Luis, will you walk with me to my next class. I really want to talk to you." No, no, no, don't do it. You know that you will start talking to her again if you do it and you can't let that happen. Keep her safe. That's what you told yourself you needed to do, do it now. I keep repeating that in my head, but when I look into her pleading eyes I know that I can't say no to her.

"Sure of course." Moron.

Walking beside her, we head to her next class while I curse myself in my head for giving in so easily. Why am I such an idiot?

"I've missed you a lot Luis. It feels as if I haven't seen you in ages." I lower my head, not wanting to see the pain in her face.

"Yeah it has been a while since we last talked."

"Have you been avoiding me because of those rumors everyone is spreading about me and the Crow?" I can hear her voice breaking. Looking back up at her, I can see tears forming in her bright blue eyes. The strong face I had been trying to keep up completely crumbles at the sight of her tears as I let my real feelings show.

"No, no I would never do that Colomba." I say this to her and it almost sounds like I'm pleading with her, begging her to believe me. She looks away from me, closing her eyes tightly as a single tear falls down her face.

"Then why did you leave me? I've missed you so much Luis. I've needed you but you weren't there. I have felt so alone these past few weeks with everything going on." I can't tell her the whole truth since I know it would hurt her. How could I tell her that I have avoided her because I don't want someone she thinks of as a friend, Alex, to turn on her and treat her like he does me? I can't break her heart like that. Instead, I only tell her part of the truth.

"I got in trouble with someone and I didn't want you to get involved. It wasn't anything you did, I can promise you that. It was all because of me." She looks back up at me, her tears now beginning to disappear.

"You could have told me Luis and I would have tried to help. I could have done something for you." I smile at her a bit weakly, feeling guilty for lying to her. I feel even worse since she wants to help me even though I basically abandoned her when she really needed me.

"You already had your own problems to deal with. I didn't want to make it any worse for you with including you in mine. Please believe me. I would never do anything to hurt you, ever." She nods her head in understanding.

"I see… are you- are you going to keep

avoiding me or is it all over? Can we be friends again?" Now my smile is real.

"Of course we can." She smiles warmly at me as we both walk to class. We start talking with each other, telling each other everything that has been going on over the past few weeks since we last talked. I feel better than I have in weeks, but that doesn't last long. Of course, my happiness never lasts long.

Up ahead of us I can see Alex leaning against a locker. His eyes are glued to Colomba and I, his evil smirk on his face. From the glimmer in his eyes I can tell that he has something stirring in his mind. A chill runs up and down my spine as I see that smirk. Something is going to happen, and something soon. I don't know what it will be, but I know it will be terrible.

The two of us walk past him and the chill that was going up and down my spine is now a block of ice on my back. He is going to do something horrible, but what really scares me is that it might not happen to me. Colomba had been standing right next to me when he smiled at us like that. He may try to hurt her too because she has started talking to me again. This is just what I was trying to prevent. I need to protect her no matter what. She can't be hurt for my mistake. I embarrassed Alex; his revenge should only hurt me. I am responsible, she is innocent. She should never be hurt because of anything that I have done.

Chapter Eleven
Colomba-
A Terrible
Truth

Even though the rumors about me are still being spread like wildfire all throughout the school, I still feel a lot better knowing that one of my best friends has come back to me. I don't think I can ever put into words how wonderful it feels knowing that I have Luis as a friend again. It is so nice to hear his voice, his laugh, to see him smile. These past few weeks without him have been the worst. I have only known him for a short time, but now I feel like I can't live without him. Whenever he is around it almost feels as if nothing bad could ever happen. I just feel so safe around him.

He came back to me just yesterday, yet we both act as if he never left. It feels as if he has always been with me. I have completely forgiven him for what happened. I know that he is a real friend to me. He wouldn't leave me alone like that unless it was for a really good reason. He may not have fully explained what that reason was, but I don't care.

I'm just happy that he is back in my life. The rest of the day after he came back to me, Luis was almost always by my side. It was almost as if he was trying to keep guard over me, to protect me from something. I have no idea what he would protect me from though. Perhaps he feels as if he should try and help me whenever someone will try and mess with me again because of these rumors. Who knows, but who cares? I have my friend back and that's all that matters.

I have just stepped out of the gym's changing room and I head over to the crowd in the center of the room that is waiting for the coach to start the class. As soon as I get close to the group most of the conversations immediately die as people stare at me with open hatred and disgust. My skin crawls seeing so much negativity being directed at me. To avoid their eyes I kneel down and start tying my shoe, pretending that I don't see their eyes burning into me. I have always hated the feeling of having people stare at me, it makes me feel like I'm some tiny thing under a microscope being examined.

"Hey Colomba, there's something I really need to tell you." I look up from my shoes to stare at Alex. I'm surprised by how serious he sounds. He never acts serious. When I look at his face I can see that he doesn't have the confident grin he usually has whenever I see him. By looking into his eyes I can tell that what is on his mind is very important.

"What is it Alex?" He looks away from me for a moment and bites his lip. From that I know that he is about to tell me something I won't like.

He always does that when he does something I don't like and is trying to make up for it. I guess he is already feeling a bit guilty for what he is about to say.

"Well the last time that the Crow attacked, I saw something that really surprised me. I haven't said anything about it to anyone, but I thought you should know since I see you hang out with him a lot." He pauses and I know that he wants me to ask him what he means, he wants to pull me deeper into the conversation. I know this, but I am so curious that I let myself fall into his trap.

"Who Alex? What are you talking about?" I see him try to hide a smile when he sees how curious I am. He hides his smile quickly to bring back his worried expression.

"Well I saw someone quickly run into the janitor's closet, and a few minutes later the Crow came out. I didn't see anybody else except them go into that closet. I know that they have to be the Crow, there's nobody else it could be." My heart is pounding in my chest so hard that it feels like it's going to pop out at any second. If he can tell me the name of the Crow then I can find them and talk to them. I can end all of this peacefully sooner than I had hoped for. I can finally stop worrying about the Crow possessing someone else and hurting people. Wait though, didn't Alex say that I hang out with this person he's talking about? Is one of my own friends the Crow? In my excitement I lose my patience with him.

"*Tell me who it is Alex.*" I say this in a very harsh tone, but Alex doesn't seem to mind. He's just happy that he has my full attention. He has my attention, just like how he always wants it. He leans in closer until his mouth is right next to my ear so that he can whisper the terrible truth.

"Luis is the Crow." My heart had been pounding a moment ago, but now it has completely stopped in my terror. What? Luis is the Crow? Suddenly, it all makes sense. The way he would always get mad whenever I would say something mean about the Crow, how he always wanted me to join sides with him, and why the Crow saved me when the Sprinter attacked. Now it all makes sense. I look up at Alex who isn't smiling, yet he still looks pretty proud of himself for some reason as he stares at me in my distress.

"Are you sure Alex? Are you sure it was Luis you saw?" He lowers his gaze from mine, the proud expression no longer on his face, as if he's hiding it.

"Yeah, I'm sure. I can't believe it either. I mean, we have been friends for years. I never would have expected him to do something evil like that. He always seemed like such a nice guy, but I guess the truly evil people know how to hide what they truly are." I look away from him, staring down at my shoes in disbelief. I can't believe this. Would Luis do something like this? I feel Alex's arm wrap around my shoulders, and he holds me close.

"Don't worry Colomba, everything will be alright. I'll make sure of that for you. You don't have to worry about a thing. I'll take care of you. I'll keep you safe." Usually I would get angry at him and get out of his grip since he thinks that I need to be taken care of, but I don't do that now. Right now it feels nice to have the comforting touch of a friend, to know that I have someone on my side that I can trust. I let him hold me as he comforts me while my mind is swirling with thoughts of Luis and the Crow.

Is Luis really the Crow? Why would he do this to me, to everyone? Why would he want to hurt this entire school? I think back to what the Crow had said when I had first fought him, when he first revealed himself. He said that everyone needed to pay for what they had done to him. Have people been doing terrible things to Luis that I don't know about? Have people been hurting my friend and he doesn't trust me enough to tell me about it? Have I been betrayed by own friend?

Only moments ago I had been thinking about how safe I feel whenever I am around Luis. Right now though, I am starting to doubt that. If he is the Crow then why is he still my friend even though I openly hate the Crow and have told him multiple times? The Crow seems like an unstable person, if Luis is the Crow wouldn't he have done something to me after I have insulted the Crow so many times? He did get a bit upset, but nothing terrible like I would have expected the Crow to do. He probably would have transformed into the Crow right then and sent his demon dogs to attack me or possessed somebody to do it for him. I don't know what to believe right now. I had felt so sure and happy only a few minutes ago. Why does everything feel so frightening now?

As the coach comes over to the group and starts

the class, Alex holds me closer as my entire world seems to fall apart around me. I feel lost when I had finally felt found again.

Chapter Twelve
Luis-
One More Reason
To Hate

I make my way to art class with joy in my heart for the first time in weeks. I'm finally able to hang out with my friends again. Truthfully, I feel a bit stupid for avoiding them in the first place. I know that I wanted to protect them from whatever Alex has planned for his revenge against me, but I know that Colomba needs me right now and I want to help her in any way I can. I can't really help her if I am avoiding her now can I?

As I turn a corner to head to class I see a familiar face and I smile.

"Hey Colomba!" I call out to her and I see her lift her head and look right at me, but she doesn't return my smile. In fact, she quickly lowers her head and practically runs away from me and down a different hall. My smile is now long gone. What the heck just happened with her?

I am stuck standing in that spot for an entire minute in shock until the warning bell rings, signaling that I will be late to class soon. This snaps me out of my shock and I rush to make it to the art room, making it just in time before the final bell rings.

Sitting down in my seat, I pull out my sketchbook and open it up to the page of the demon dog that I am finishing up for this week's project. Even though I had been eager to complete the picture today only a few moments ago, now I can't even be bothered to pick up my pencil to finish sketching it. What caused Colomba to run away from me like that? She was completely fine with me just earlier this morning, why did she feel like she needed to run away from me? I bury my face in my hands as I try to think of an answer to those questions, but nothing comes in my head. I feel as if I am losing my friend all over again, but this time she is the one abandoning me, not the other way around.

While my face is still in my hands, even though my eyes are covered, I can still hear someone walk over to me and stand in front of my desk. The all too familiar feeling that something bad is about to happen comes over me and a chill runs down my spine. A sinister, dark chuckle comes from in front of me and I know who it is without looking.

"Wow don't you look pathetic." Alex practically laughs out loud at my misery. "You look as if you just found out the world is ending. You know, I actually feel a bit bad for you." I look up at Alex, completely confused. When has he ever felt bad for me? If he did ever feel bad for me then he wouldn't pick on me so much.

"What are you talking about?" Alex chuckles another one of his evil chuckles as he smiles down at me as if he holds a secret that he knows that I want.

"Well I mean about you and Colomba." I feel my eyes grow wide in surprise. "She's never going to talk to you now. I mean after she found out who you really are, she was so upset. I mean, she couldn't even speak for a few minutes she was so mortified. I felt a little guilty about having to tell her, but I knew that she had to know. It was only right; she should know something like that." I feel my hands clenching into fists on top of my desk. Is he the reason why Colomba avoided me like that in the hallway? Is he trying to ruin the only real friendship I have? What does he mean by "who I really am"? What does he think he knows about me?

"What are you talking about Alex?" The evil glimmer in his eyes just seems to grow brighter when he sees my pain.

"I'm talking about how Colomba now knows that you're the Crow." My anger suddenly leaves me and my heart stops beating. What did he just say? He knows that I'm the Crow? He knows and he told Colomba? How does he know? I look back up at Alex to see that he is still smiling down at me, that's when it hits me. He really doesn't know. If he knew I was the Crow he wouldn't be gloating like this, he would be running scared since he knows that the Crow wants to make all of the people like him pay for what they have done. He just told Colomba that I am the Crow since he knows how much she hates the Crow and he knew that she would hate me too if she thought that I am the Crow. More hatred than I have ever felt in my life boils in my stomach as I look at Alex. I know why he did this. He has finally gotten his revenge on me for tripping him in that mud puddle and having everyone laugh at him a few weeks ago. He didn't do anything like beating me up like he usually does, instead he hurt me in a way I never even thought of. He hurt me in my heart.

Alex walks away from me, smiling in victory as he walks back to his friends who all give him high fives for defeating me once again. I stare down at the picture of the demon dog on my paper and I have a sudden urge to find a quiet place where I can be alone so that I can transform in the Crow. I want to send an entire army of my dogs after him. I want to make him regret everything he has ever done to me. I want him to know what true pain is. I want to do all of that, but I know I can't. I can't do something like that.

The entire class seems to pass like eternity as I stare down at my drawing, but I never even pick up my pencil. I stare at the picture as my heart seems to shatter in my chest in a million pieces and I don't know if it can ever be fixed. I am miserable, while Alex and his friends are laughing and joking around only a few feet away from me. Just like always, Alex has defeated me.

Chapter Thirteen
Colomba- Defending Rosie

I walk through the halls with my head hanging low. This class period is study hall for me, so I am using the time to go to the library and get something to read. As I pass by a door leading outside to the courtyard in the center of the school I see something that makes me stop in my tracks.

Within the courtyard I see that girl I met the other day, Rosie. She is kneeling down beside a flowerbed and is tending to the brightly colored flowers with a loving hand. I have heard that the school lets her use her study hall time to tend to the flowers and other plants around the school since she is such an expert on them, and the school also gives her a little bit of money for her work. Honestly, I don't think she really cares about the money she just wants to be with the plants. I guess the school wants to help her feel a bit happier here since the school has been unable to stop any of the bullies from messing with her.

As I watch her clip off the dead branches of a red rose bush I see two boys enter the courtyard and start walking down the sidewalk toward Rosie, who has her back turned toward them. One of them nudges his friend and points at Rosie. The feeling I always get whenever something bad is about to happen goes crazy and I quickly run to the door to get to Rosie, but it is too late. The boy who had nudged his friend sneaks up behind Rosie and then quickly leaps up and lands hard on a tulip plant right next to her.

Rosie lets out a shriek of horror as the boy grinds his feet over the crushed flower while the two boys laugh at her. Tears stream down her face as I rush over to her and wrap my arms around her as she bawls uncontrollably. All I have to do is glare at those two guys and they hurry back into the school, leaving me and Rosie alone. They probably left so quickly because they were afraid of me. With all the rumors floating around about how I'm partnered with the Crow they probably thought that if they stayed I might call the Crow and make trouble for them. It's nice to know that these rumors have done at least one good thing for me.

The front of my shirt is now soaked from Rosie's tears as I hold her close, rubbing her back gently, trying to comfort her.

"It's alright Rosie, it's alright." I try to say over her sobs, but this only causes her to wail louder in my arms.

"They killed my friend!" She practically screams into my shoulder. I glance down at the flower that the cruel boy had stomped on.

"No, they didn't. Look closer." I point toward the wounded flower and her eyes eagerly look at it, hoping that I have not lied to her about her "friend" not being dead. "Look, see the flower may be broken off now and a few leaves torn, but it is still alive, and it will grow again. I know that with you helping it, the flower will grow back stronger than before." Rosie nods her head and tries to smile through her tears.

"Yes, my friend will come back." She uses a set of clippers that she had been using on the rose bush to clip the broken leaves and flower stems from the plant. From my experience in gardening with my grandmother, I know that by cutting off these dead parts she is helping the plant heal.

Rosie doesn't even look at me anymore, she is now completely absorbed in caring for her injured friend. I smile softly, a little amused by how quickly her emotions had changed from uncontrollable terror and sadness back to a relaxed composure. I pick myself off the ground and walk back inside to head to the library again. When I make it there, I take my time browsing through the shelves of books. As I wander through the massive shelves I think about Rosie.

I have heard her parents talk to my grandmother about how their daughter gets picked on a lot in school. They have even told her a few stories about what some of the other kids have done to her. They would like to send her to a different school so that she might get treated better, but they can't afford something like that, so Rosie is practically stuck here in this school where people hurt and tease her.

They once told my grandmother about how some students had filled Rosie's locker with notes calling her stupid, a moron, or anything else they could think of. Her parents reported this to the school, but nobody was ever caught so nothing ever happened. I don't think that there is anything more frustrating than knowing that you can't do anything to help your child, no matter how much pain they are in. I want to help her too, but how can I help her when I can't even help myself? Right now people are making fun of me constantly and avoiding me like I've got the plague. How can I help Rosie with her bullying problem if mine is just as bad, or even worse, right now?

In my frustration I pick out a book at random and check it out from the librarian before rushing out to head back to study hall. My mind is running through so many questions as I make my way through the halls. It seems that a thousand different questions pass in the few minutes it takes to make it to the classroom, but the one that keeps returning in my mind is what am I going to do?

Chapter Fourteen
Luis-
Hoping for
Forgiveness

When the final bell has rung, and everyone is heading out the front doors to either head to a car or bus to take them home, I am not searching for my bus along with everyone else. I am looking for Colomba. Because of that stupid, cruel Alex, Colomba now thinks that I am the Crow. I **am** the Crow, but I didn't want her to find that out now. I was hoping that she would find that out later. After I've convinced her that I'm not the bad guy but, thanks to Alex, she now thinks I am the bad guy.

I frantically try to find her in the crowd so that I can catch her before she gets on the bus. I know that when she gets on the bus she can easily find a seat in a crowded spot so that I can't get near her, or she will have her friend Nat keep me away from her, and I need to explain myself to her. I will have to lie to her and tell her that I am not the Crow. It hurts me to know that I will have to lie to her, but, more than anything, I want her to stay my friend. If it means that I have to lie to keep her as a friend then I will do that. I won't let Alex, or anyone else, get in the way of my friendship with her. Isn't it okay to lie to keep a friend when you're as desperate as me to have a friend?

Since I am so tall it is kind of easy to see over everyone's heads to search for her. As I search through the crowd it looks as if I am glancing over a sea of hair and faces. None of these nameless faces really mean anything to me, all except one that I spot only a dozen feet away from me. I rush through the crowd until I make it to her side.

"Hey Colomba." She glances up at me for a moment, but once she sees who she is looking at, her eyes fall again. She stares down at her shoes and practically whispers her greeting to me.

"Oh, hi Luis." She almost looks like she's scared to be talking to me, as if I might attack her at any minute. It physically hurts to see her look at me like this. It feels like I'm being stabbed in my heart.

"Listen, I heard about what Alex said to you and I just needed to say that it's not true. I'm not the Crow. I promise I'm not." She glances up at me from the corner of her eye.

"Honestly Luis, I have a problem believing that." I am stunned by her words. Why is she doubting me? Does she really believe what Alex says over what I say?

"Why?" She turns completely toward me so that she can face me, her eyes burning in rage.

"Because it would make sense!" Her small hands are balled up into fists at her side in her anger. "You have always been on the side of the

Crow and you used to keep trying to convince me to join the Crow's side too. We would even get into arguments about the Crow because you kept trying to make me change my mind about him. Doesn't it make sense that you would be the Crow?" I can't help but see her logic. I do seem like the most likely one who would be the Crow. Dang it! How do I convince her that I'm not the Crow when I really am the Crow? Life *really* sucks sometimes!

"I know that you think it's true, but I swear it's not. I'm not the Crow. *Please* believe me." She stares into my eyes for what feels like ages, as if she is hoping that she can read my thoughts if she looks into my eyes long enough.

"I wish I could." Without another word she walks away from me and steps on the bus with Nat following right after her. Nat gives her a warm smile and tries to cheer Colomba up considering she looks pretty miserable. I may not be able to be with her now, but I'm glad that Colomba has Nat. At least she has a friend who wants to cheer her up whenever she looks sad. I'm sure that Colomba will explain to Nat why she is so miserable and why she just dismissed me, then Nat will make sure that I stay as far away from them as possible.

I hang my head as I get on the bus too, but I sit alone today. I have a feeling that I am going to have to get used to sitting alone again considering what just happened. I try to get rid of these depressing thoughts by reading a book, but not even that can help me. I stare out the window and watch the world pass by as the bus makes its way through town while my heart seems to break with each mile that passes.

Chapter Fifteen
Colomba-
Finally Telling
Grandma

The bus ride home seems to take forever. When I step off the bus and start walking down the driveway toward my house I feel a sense of relief, knowing that I am finally away from all of those people who seem to hate me. When I enter through the front door I sigh, feeling safe at last.

"Hello, anybody home?!" I cry out, and it barely takes a second before my question is answered.

"Hello Tesoro. How is my favorite girl?" My grandma comes in from the living room and gives me one of her warm, sweet hugs. Once I am out of her embrace she looks me in the face and her smile immediately disappears. "Why, what has happened my love, you look as if you want to cry?" I lower my eyes, not wanting her to see the pain I've been trying so hard to keep from her.

"It's nothing. I'm alright." She gently lifts

my chin so that I am looking her in the eyes.

"Tesoro, I'm an old woman. I have enough experience to know that something is wrong, now tell me." I can't help myself, after holding in my emotions and keeping it a secret from her for so long, I tell her everything. The tears just keep going down my face as I tell her about how everyone is treating me like an outcast because of what the Crow did when the Sprinter attacked and how most of my friends have abandoned me.

"I am so sorry that this has happened Tesoro. It must be such a terrible feeling to be so alone." I sniffle a little as I wipe my nose on my cardigan sleeve.

"It's not that bad. At least I still have Nat and Alex by my side." Grandma looks at me strangely after that, as if she's worried about something that I just said.

"Is Alex the one that you have been telling me about, the friend who compliments you too much and flirts with you whenever he can?" I can feel my cheeks burning and I know that I am blushing furiously.

"Yes." I practically whisper in my embarrassment.

"I wouldn't trust him if I were you. A man like that shouldn't be trusted. Men who compliment too much are usually out to get something from you. I know that it may seem nice to have him by your side now when everything looks so bleak, but make sure that he doesn't get too close to you. You may regret it afterward." I nod my head.

"I understand, but he is so nice to me and I

don't want to lose one of the only friends I have left." She nods too, understanding how I feel.

"Is there anything I can do to help?" I close my eyes, feeling completely helpless.

"No, not really. The Crow was right about something, nobody really helps the bullied kids in school. The other students join in, the teachers don't do anything to stop them, and the people in charge of the school don't care until something really bad happens, then all they do is make a few speeches and make everything seem fixed when it's really not. If you go in to talk to anybody at the school, they won't do anything. When they find out why I'm getting picked on they probably wouldn't want to help anyway. The teachers hate the Crow just as much as most of the students. If they think I'm his little helper too they won't want to help me either. I don't really know what we can do." She holds me close and it feels as if some of my problems have already melted away. Grandma has always had that gift, making me feel better with a simple hug.

"Don't worry Tesoro. I know that things will work out. People will realize that you aren't siding with him and things will go back to normal. I just know it. Just stay strong and everything will turn out well." I want to tell her that I've been strong the past few weeks, but things have only gotten worse, but I don't. I don't want to worry her any more than I already have. Instead of telling her the truth, I tell her about another problem that is happening in my life.

"There is something else that is worrying me."

"What is it Tesoro?" I look down at my shoes,

unsure of how to say this.

"Do you remember how I told you yesterday that Luis had started talking to me again?" She nods as she smiles. She always smiles when I talk about Luis. My grandma has never met Luis, but from everything that I have said about him she has grown to like him. "Well earlier today I heard something that kind of terrifies me. Alex said that when the Crow attacked the school the last time, he saw Luis walk into a closet and a moment later the Crow came out and started creating trouble. Luis might be the Crow." Grandma falls silent for a minute or two as she thinks about what I just said. It feels like forever before she responds to what I just said.

"You said that Alex is the one who told you this?" I nod my head at her. "And he decided to tell you this now, a few weeks after the Crow attacked, only a day after you started talking to Luis again?" I nod again, a bit more hesitantly though. Where is she going with this? She appears uncomfortable right now, as if she really doesn't want to say what she thinks but knows that she has to to help me. "Do you think that Alex might have just made that up to get Luis out of the way?" My eyes narrow in confusion as I look at her, trying to understand what she means.

"What are you talking about?" She sighs softly.

"Well this boy, Alex, seems to like you a great deal and would be willing to do anything to be around you. Don't you think it would be possible that he made that story up so that you would stop hanging out with another boy, Luis, so that he could have your full attention?" I am stunned into silence by her words. She really thinks that Alex would lie to me just to have my full attention, getting Luis out of the way? She has never even met Alex, how could someone as kind as my grandmother think so negatively of a person she has never even met?

"A- Alex would never do that. I mean he is a bit rough around the edges, but he is a good person. I'm sure of it." She looks away from me again, once again uncomfortable.

"Tesoro, your father and I have tried very hard to give you a good life, a life with very little pain and suffering. Due to this, you have grown into a young lady who is very innocent to how the world is. You must learn to recognize when someone may be doing something against you for their own interests, like how I believe this boy, Alex, may be doing to you now. I do not want you to lose a friend when he may have not done anything wrong and have you fall into the hands of a boy who is willing to lie to get what he wants." I look away from her too, afraid of what she has just said. Was Alex lying to me just so I wouldn't hang out with Luis and hang out with him more? I mean I did hang out with him a lot more when Luis was avoiding me. Since he knew that I had made up with Luis that would make him think that I wouldn't be hanging out as much with him anymore. We had been getting a lot closer recently, and by getting close to Luis that may threaten what may have started happening between Alex and I. Alex may have recognized this and decided to lie to make sure that wouldn't happen.

I start thinking through this, but I force it out of

my mind. I can't think this way. I have always tried to see the best in people, not the worst. Alex wouldn't lie to me. Maybe the person he saw who transformed into the Crow wasn't Luis, maybe he just thought it was. On the other hand, maybe what he saw was right and the Crow really is Luis. I don't know what the answer is, and this is really confusing me. I just don't know what to believe anymore. This all just feels like a tangled web that I am stuck in the middle of.

"I don't know what to do Grandma. I don't know who I should believe." She smiles at me, trying to make me feel better in this strange situation.

"I'm sure that you will figure out the right thing to do. As I have said many times, you are a very smart young lady and you will know who to believe when the time is right. Don't worry, everything will be fine." I smile at her, wanting to say the truth, but instead I give a little lie.

"I'm sure that things will work out too. I'm going to head to the backyard and practice some martial arts a little bit before dinner." I head to my room to grab my practice weapons and then quickly go into my backyard. I want to go to the backyard to practice because I want to be alone. I don't want my grandma to see just how miserable I really feel.

Opening my practice weapon bag, I pull out my practice sword that I use when I practice how to use the katana, or Japanese sword. This practice weapon is made of solid wood and is shaped like a sword. It is called a bokken, and when practicing with this with other people you still have to be careful even though it isn't a real sword. I should know this; I have been hit with one by accident a few times and it is extremely painful. Since it's made of solid wood it feels like you're getting hit with a large stick, not pleasant.

I slice through the empty air with the practice sword, moving across the ground silently as I slash through invisible enemies. With each step I start moving faster and faster, my frustration with everything going on making my swings of the sword harder and full of anger. My invisible enemies fall quickly at my well-trained hands. I cut through them all, pretending that they are my problems, pretending that they are all of the negativity in my head. This usually helps me feel better, pretending to slash apart my problems, but not today. As I cut through one problem after another my anger just seems to increase.

My heart races and my muscles tense as I feel my fury grow. My grip on the handle of my practice sword is so tight that my knuckles have turned white. I know that I should stop and try to make myself relax, but I don't want to stop. I want to release this rage. I think about every single person who has laughed, teased, and avoided me ever since this began. I didn't do anything to them and yet they have hurt me almost constantly for weeks.

For those who use katanas, whenever you practice, when you swing the sword you want it to make a kind of whooshing sound, that way you know that you are swinging at the correct angle and with the right amount of force. The lower the pitch of the whooshing sound, the better the swing. If you get it just right it sounds like the wind is rushing past you. With my level of training, the air is full of that strange sound. Just from listening I know that I am doing well in my practice, but that doesn't help me cheer up either. My heart feels like it is breaking.

Tears are beginning to fall down my face, but I still swing the sword. My arms are starting to get sore from overworking them, but I still don't stop. My thoughts shift from how people have been hurting me to start thinking about everything I have seen people do to Rosie. Rosie should never be picked on, she was born the way she is, but nobody shows her mercy. They hurt her without a second thought. I didn't think it was possible, but my rage only seems to grow. I release a battle cry full of all my pain as I lift my sword to cut downward. Turning around I swing the sword down with all my might and a terrible cracking sound echoes through my backyard. I stare down in horror at what I did. In my hands is now the shattered remains of my wooden practice sword. In my rage I wasn't paying attention and I had accidently hit my sword against a large rock, causing it to break apart.

The tears flow down my face as I stare at the ruined remains of my beloved weapon. I have had this practice weapon for years and now I have ruined it. This one always seemed to work well for me and practicing with it in the backyard has helped me work out a lot of pain before. Sadly, today the pain finally beat this poor little broken thing in my hands. With tears still in my eyes, I pick up the shattered bits of my weapon and take them inside, avoiding the kitchen since my grandma is in there and I don't want her to see what I have done. I suddenly feel ashamed with myself for letting my rage control me and make me do something like that to an item I really loved. Now I will have to carve a new one, and that could take a really long time to make it just the way I like it.

I don't stop moving until I have made it to my room. There I place the shattered pieces of my practice sword and place them on the ground, staring down at them pitifully. As I look down at the pieces I think about what I can do. I don't want to just throw this away; it has meant a lot to me and it would seem almost ungrateful to this practice sword to just treat it like garbage after all of the happiness it has given me.

A sudden idea comes to me and I choose the biggest shard of wood and set it on my dresser while throwing the remaining pieces away. As soon as I can, I will make something amazing out of that to always remember my weapon from, the weapon I destroyed. The guilt washes over me again along with the rage that had momentarily disappeared when I broke my weapon. It's all because of those people at school. They're the ones who upset me and caused me to break my practice sword. I lower my head in shame, I can't blame them for what I did. I am responsible for my actions, no one else. I quickly go into the bathroom to take a shower before dinner. As the hot water washes over me I let the tears out that I had been holding in. With the water falling around me I know that nobody in my house will be able to hear my sobbing, here I am safe to release my emotions without causing my grandma and dad to get worried. I cry until I feel as if I have no tears left in me. That didn't take too long, I have already cried so much recently that it's surprising that I had any tears left at all.

As soon as I am through, I force myself to get out of the shower and get dressed so that I can go to dinner and pretend like everything is alright so that I won't worry my father. I haven't told him about what I have been going through recently and I hope he won't find out. Dad has always been very protective of me, if he finds out what has been going on then he might try to contact the school to make them do something about this but that never ends well. Whenever a parent calls to tell the school about their child getting picked on it usually makes everything worse for their kid. I don't want him to get involved in this. I don't want him to share my pain. I would rather suffer alone. I smile warmly at my grandma and dad as I meet them at the dinner table, and we have a pleasant conversation while I feel like I am still crying on the inside.

Chapter Sixteen
Luis-
A New
Possibility

The afternoon sun streams in through the windows as I make my way through the school halls to head for the bus to go home. Even though it is a beautiful day outside it feels so gloomy around me. I feel so bad knowing that one of my only friends thinks I am a monster. That is just one small way of ruining a person's day.

As I turn down one hallway I see a familiar face and I break out into a sprint to catch up to them.

"Colomba, I really need to talk to you." She walks past me, her eyes looking down at the ground, avoiding my gaze.

"I don't want to talk about it anymore Luis. Please, I just want to be alone to think about all of this. All I have to go on is what you and Alex have said, and I honestly don't know who to believe. Just give me some time to think please."

"What's there to think about!? You know I

would never hurt anybody while Alex would hurt anybody to get what he wants!" This gets Colomba to turn and face me with anger in her eyes.

"That's a terrible thing to say about Alex!" I want to shake my head in pity and tell her everything that I have ever seen him do to people, but I don't want to break her innocence. Also that would take all day and we have to get to the bus before it leaves.

"But it's true. He's only nice to you because he thinks you're pretty!" Her anger immediately disappears to be replaced by pain and I instantly feel guilty for what I just said.

"He's my friend Luis, and I'm sure he would still like me even if I wasn't pretty. You can't say that about people when you don't really know what's going on in their heads. He likes hanging out with me, he likes talking to me." Her voice cracks when she says this, as if she is holding back tears right now.

"I didn't mean to hurt you Colomba, I really didn't, but please just listen to me. I can explain everything." She holds her hand up in front of me in a stopping gesture.

"I don't want to hear it right now Luis, as I said a minute ago, I want some time to think. Don't push it." With that said, she marches away from me down the hall. As I watch her walk away another person comes up beside her and walks next to her. My rage rises as I see him smile at her.

"Hey Colomba, how are you doing?" Alex asks with his usual confident grin on his face. When Colomba smiles back up at him it feels as if a knife has stabbed me in the heart. Her smile is full of kindness and warmth, the way she used to smile at me.

"I'm okay. How are you?" His already large grin gets bigger as he wraps his arm around her shoulders. My eyes grow wide in shock as I see him holding her close. A little bit of hope sparks inside me as I think that she will just move away from him or even hit him for touching her like that. I keep watching them, hoping to see the look of disappointment and misery on Alex's face when she turns him down.

"I'm always good when I'm with you." I watch with horror as she lets Alex's arm stay around her. She's letting him hold her? It feels as if the world has disappeared around me, all except Alex and Colomba walking down the hall together. Nothing exists but them. As they continue walking, Alex turns his head back around to look at me and give me a triumphant smirk before he turns his attention back on Colomba. It feels like someone just sucker punched me in the gut. All the air has left my lungs and yet it is difficult to breathe. I want to cry, but everyone in this school already thinks I'm a wimp, so I hold that back to keep them from laughing at me like they always do. If I cry in front of everyone then I will just be made fun of worse than I already am for about a week or two. I should know I've had plenty of experience with this.

Instead of releasing my emotions like I really want to, I head to the bus and sit down in the first empty seat I can find and press my face against the window. I make sure that nobody can see my face, so that none of them can see the tears that are beginning to fall down my face. The tears make a streak down the window my face is pressed against, creating a strange pattern with my tears on the glass. When I look at it, the pattern kind of looks like a sad puppy or something like that. The puppy matches me.

When the bus stops in front of my uncle's shop I grab my backpack and run out so that nobody can see that my face is red and puffy from crying. I don't even stop to say hi to my Uncle Diego, who is placing a tea set inside an antique cabinet. Instead, I run into our apartment upstairs and head straight for my room. As soon as the door is closed I place my hand over my medal so that Shadow appears in front of me, perched on top of my dresser.

"Good afternoon Master." She states with her usually pleasant voice, but I don't waste any time with pleasantries, I get straight down to business.

"Did you see the way that Alex had his arm around her?! I could have transformed into the Crow on the spot and sent my dogs to rip him apart! He would have deserved it! He would have deserved everything I could have done to him!" I pace my room, filled with a crazy energy in my rage.

"Yes I did see that Master. It must have been very distressing for you." Shadow states, still so calm despite how angry I am. "I could feel your pain when you saw that, but you and I both know that hurting Alex would only make things worse." I shake my head.

"Of course I know that, but I want…I want-"

"What do you want?"

"I want to convince Colomba that I'm not the Crow!"

"But you are the Crow." Shadow replies sarcastically. I glare at her as my hands ball into fists at my sides.

"I know that." I growl at her. "I just need to make sure that she doesn't know that until she starts thinking of the Crow as the good guy, then I want her to know who I am. Until then though that has to be a complete secret. I don't want her to ever suspect me." Shadow nods silently in deep thought.

"Well there might be one way that you could do that." My anger suddenly vanishes as I look at Shadow with hope.

"How?! Tell me! *Please* tell me!" She fluffs out her feathers and sticks her beak in the air, something she does whenever she is saying something that she's not quite sure about.

"If Colomba sees you as yourself while one of the Crow's soldiers is in the school, then she might think that you're not the Crow." I nod my head.

"So, you think that if she sees me as myself, Luis, while someone I have given superpowers is attacking the school then she might think I'm not the Crow?" Shadow nods at me.

"Exactly." I smile seeing the brilliance of that.

"That sounds like a fantastic idea Shadow, but I didn't know that I could leave my form as the Crow while someone I have given superpowers is still running around getting their revenge." Shadow flies off my dresser to land on my shoulder.

"It is possible, but a very difficult thing to do. You will need all of your concentration to make sure that the person still has those powers and won't fade once you transform back into your normal self. Only a few people who have had my medal before have ever been able to master that skill. You will have to be able to focus not only on what you are doing, but also what the person you have transformed is doing You are a very intelligent young man though, and a very determined one as well, so I think that you will be able to do it with a little bit of effort." I am so happy right now that I could kiss Shadow on her beak, but that would be pretty weird for the both of us so thankfully I am able to control myself.

"Alright Shadow, tell me exactly how I can do that."

<u>Chapter Seventeen</u>
Colomba-
It All Gets
Worse

Well out of all the days since everyone started treating me like dirt this day hasn't been that bad. Alex was so kind to me in gym earlier today. I told him about how upset I was when I told my grandma about what has been happening and he held me close as he told me that everything will be alright. He said that he will make everyone stop hurting me. He is such a nice guy. I have no idea why Luis and Grandma keep warning me about him. It doesn't make sense. Why should I stay away from someone who has always been so nice to me? Oh well, they don't know everything so maybe they're wrong about him. Who knows?

Turning down the hall to head to my next class, I smile when I see Rosie walking toward me. That smile quickly fades though when I see that somebody else is near her, someone that can erase the smile on anybody's face, Angela. Rosie is looking down at a piece of paper, examining something written on it. Angela notices this too and snatches the paper from her hands and starts reading it while Rosie looks at her in fear, knowing that whatever will happen will be terrible.

"What is this?" Angela laughs as she stares at the paper. ""My One- Hundred Favorite Flowers", you actually made a list of something that stupid?!" Angela laughs at her cruelly while a few people who overheard her start laughing along with her. "How pathetic is your life that you even think about making a list like this?" Rosie lowers her head and lets her hair hang in front of her face, trying to hide herself from the world, but that doesn't stop me from seeing a tear beginning to fall down her face. Angela smirks at her, enjoying the fact that she has made Rosie look so defeated.

"What are you looking down for? Look at me! Look me in the eyes you freak!" Rosie doesn't do this though; she keeps her head down with fear. I know that with people with Asperger's usually have trouble looking people in the eyes or acting in a way that most people would expect, and I think that Angela knows this too, that is why she is rubbing it in. "You can't do that can you? Can you, you little dumb freak?"

Rushing over to them, I grab the list and take it from Angela before giving it back to Rosie. I give Rosie a quick, reassuring smile before I turn back to face Angela, glaring at her with all the anger and pain I have been keeping inside of me since everyone started making fun of me a few weeks ago.

"So what if she makes a list like that? It's

not like it affects you or anybody else. It's just something she wanted to do with her time. Don't tease someone just because they do things a little different than you." I practically growl these words to her in my frustration, but she only looks amused by me.

""A little different"? Oh please, we all know what she is Colomba! She's a freak, a dumb stupid freak. She should be in one of the special classes anyway so that she won't have to be around us and annoy me." Even the people who had been laughing along with Angela a moment ago look uncomfortable about what she just said. Many of them realize that what she is saying is wrong, but nobody dares to speak up, nobody except me. I may not have been able to help Rosie before, but I can do it now.

"You should be ashamed of yourself for saying something like that Angela." She doesn't look ashamed at all, in fact, she looks pretty proud of herself. She always looks proud of herself though. It's hard to find any other emotion on her face. I've known her for years and I can't think of any moment when she didn't look proud. "Rosie is not stupid, and she never will be. If you really want to see who the stupid one here is then look in a mirror Angela. Only an idiot like you would say such terrible things to a person who has done nothing to you." I know that what I said was mean, but I don't apologize. Instead, I take Rosie by the hand and lead her away from the astonished crowd that surrounds us and Angela, leaving them all with open- mouthed shock. They're all shocked that I am the one who said that. Nobody has ever really heard me say anything mean to anybody. Truthfully, I'm a bit shocked I said that myself. I am shocked, but I do not regret it.

Only once we have turned a corner and escaped from all of those people who had been laughing at her do I look back at Rosie to see tears falling down her face.

"It's alright Rosie. Angela always says terrible things like that to everyone. She is kind of a monster, but just know that practically everything she says is a lie." Rosie shakes her head at me as the tears continue to flow.

"She's not the only one who says that! Everyone says I'm stupid!" She is yelling and causing a scene. I don't think she really realizes that, but I don't care. All I care about is her.

"Well I don't. I think that you're a very smart girl." Rosie opens her eyes and glances up at my face for a moment, but then quickly looks back down again.

"Really?" I smile at her even though I know she can't see it since she is staring down at her shoes.

"Of course. Now tell me, what is your favorite flower, that really is what the list says doesn't it?" Rosie nods faintly.

"Yes, my favorite flower is the iris." As we continue walking to our next classes she tells me all about irises and why she loves them. She gets so happy and animated when she talks about flowers that she completely forgets about what happened and her tears disappear. It makes me happy to see her so happy. When I make it to my own class, I sit down in my chair with a smile, feeling proud of myself for what I did with Angela and Rosie. Of course, that happiness doesn't last very long.

When the class ends, I step out of the classroom with my head held high, happy that I did something good for someone else. If I had only noticed her a moment earlier it might not have happened, but I noticed a familiar face from the side and before I could react I saw a bottle of water come closer to me and all of the water inside of it splashes directly into my face.

I give out a little shriek of shock as the water sprays into my face and runs down my cheeks. Angela laughs wickedly as she runs off before any of the teachers could notice what happened. None of the other students stop her, none of them even come up to me to give me some kind of comfort. A few people laugh at me as my hair, now stringy and hanging down from the water, falls into my face. This doesn't hide the fact that I am close to tears. I know why Angela did that, she's angry about what I said to her earlier, but she made sure that she got back at me.

More people laugh at me as they watch the water drip from my chin and the ends of my hair. My tears mix with the water as I turn away from everyone and run down the hall. I think I hear someone call out my name from behind me, but I don't stop to see who it is. I run outside into the courtyard and find a secluded spot behind a corner. I practically fall next to the edge of a flowerbed that was cared for by Rosie, and the tears continue to stream down my face in torrents. I have never felt so miserable in my life. I cover my face with my hands as the tears fall without any sign of ever stopping. The water drips from my hair and onto the mulch of the flowerbed beneath me. The water almost immediately disappears as soon as it touches the mulch. Right now I wish the earth could swallow me up like that too. I want to disappear.

I hear the sound of grass being stepped on near me, but I don't look toward the sound. I keep my face hidden by my hands. A familiar voice calls out to me, sounding very distressed.

"Colomba, what's wrong?" I remove my hands from my face so that I can look at Luis with tear-filled eyes as he goes down on his knees close beside me.

"The same thing that's been happening for weeks. Everyone has turned on me! Everyone thinks that I'm partnered with the Crow or something because he saved me when the Sprinter attacked the school and a bunch of rocks fell on me. They also said that I must be dating him too since he risked so much to help me. People have been treating me like a traitor because of that. They think I'm a horrible person just because he helped me. Even though everyone hates me, I still tried to help Rosie when Angela was picking on her earlier and she sprayed me with water. I didn't even do anything! *Why are they doing this to me?!*" I look at him, hoping that he can give me an answer for my question, but he doesn't have one to give to me.

"I don't know Colomba. Nobody really knows why people do stuff like this. They just don't understand how kind you are and that you would never do anything to hurt anybody. They don't see you the way I see you." I close my eyes for a moment as the tears overflow down my face again.

"I thought that you of all people would have been happy that this has happened, that you would think that I support the Crow just like everyone else." He looks me straight in the eyes with a miserable glance.

"I could never be happy if you are miserable like this." As the tears come again, I reach out and I hold him close to me as my heart breaks. I feel his arms wrap around me too as he tries to comfort me.

Luis holds me close as my entire body shakes as I cry my eyes out. I know what Alex said about Luis, he said that he is the Crow, but I don't care. Right now, I don't care if Luis really is the Crow or not. It just feels nice having his arms around me as I cry, comforting me. I have missed my friend. I never want him to leave my side again.

Why is this happening to me? I didn't do anything so why is everyone trying to be so cruel to me? A thought enters my mind and I suddenly feel worse. Do the people the Crow transformed feel this way too? Did they feel as lost as I am? They felt lost so they decided to side with the Crow to try and make themselves feel better? As I sit here with Luis, my eyes red from my tears, I think I finally understand how they felt. I understand how much pain they felt. They believed that joining him was their only way to get rid of this pain that seems unescapable. While the pain tears away at me from the inside, I understand everything. I understand,

but it doesn't make me feel better. I don't feel better
at all.

Chapter Eighteen
Luis-
My Plan for
Colomba's Revenge

As I enter one of the hallways, I look up to see something that stops me dead in my tracks, Colomba running down the hall straight past me as water drips off of her. What just happened? Did she just jump into a pool or something? I call after her, but she doesn't even look back at me. Running after her, I follow her into the courtyard. When I make it there, she has vanished from my sight. I look around frantically, praying to find her. I do not see her, but I find her from a soft sound. It almost sounds like crying, but no she shouldn't be crying. What could have made her cry?

Turning around the corner, I am greeted by the sight that I never wanted to see, Colomba crying. She is sitting on the grass next to a bed of flowers, her back against the wall of the school. Her face is buried in her hands as I see a few tears falling down her cheeks. Rushing over to her, I go down on my knees so that I am at her level. I ask her what's wrong and she tells me that it's because of what everyone is saying about her and how Angela treated her badly. She also says that she thought that I would be happy since everyone thinks that she's on the same side as the Crow. I look her straight in the eyes and tell her the truth.

"I could never be happy if you are miserable like this." When she hears my words she breaks down into sobs again as she throws her arms around me in a tight hug. Stunned, I am frozen for a moment before I wrap my arms around her too as she shakes with her sobbing. As she cries in my arms, I think about all the people who probably just watched everything that Angela did to her and didn't do anything. They didn't help this poor innocent girl, many of them probably laughed.

I can't believe that this happened. What is wrong with these people? How could anybody hurt someone as sweet as Colomba on purpose? I have been made fun of my entire life, but I have never been angrier about the bullies in this school than I am right now. Looking down at her in my arms, I see all of the misery and pain she has been holding back this entire time since I helped her when the Sprinter attacked. Tears keep falling from her beautiful aquamarine eyes as she rests her head on my chest. Right now, I want this to never end, but I also don't. I love that I am able to hold her, but I hate that I am holding her because she is so upset. Jeez emotions are confusing.

As she silently cries in my arms one thought races through my mind. They hurt her. They hurt her… No, no they didn't hurt her. Colomba was right all along, I hurt her. I caused all of this. These rumors spread because of me since I helped her while I was the Crow. I am responsible for her pain. I am the reason that she is crying right now. It feels as if a stone has fallen into my stomach. I have never felt this guilty in my entire life.

Only a few weeks ago, I would have done anything to be able to hold Colomba like this, but now it only hurts me. I know that I am only holding her now because she needs comfort. I want to make all of her pain go away. I would take it willingly if I could, but I know I can't. I can only sit here and comfort her as she cries.

It takes a little while for her tears to dry, and class has already started, but I don't mind. I'm glad that she let me keep her company and comfort her. I walk her to her next class, but I do not walk to my own classroom after I am done. As I pass through the hallway a dark smile crawls over my face.

I may not be able to give Colomba power since she won't accept it, but maybe if I give powers to that Rosie girl that Colomba was trying to defend then maybe everyone will stop bullying each other after that and Colomba will still be safe. Genius. And then once this Rosie girl gets her revenge and scares the entire school then everyone will get what they deserve for making Colomba cry. I will make them pay.

Rosie will definitely want to get revenge after everything that has happened to her recently, as well as what people have always done to her. She will willingly accept the powers I will give her. People make fun of her just because she is autistic, they think that she is stupid because of that. Well I'm going to teach them just how stupid *they* are for thinking that way.

I go into the guy's bathroom, making sure that nobody is inside before I lock the door and place my hand over my medal so that Shadow appears on the counter.

"Hello Master, you seem to be in a good mood." I chuckle at her.

"Yes, I am. I now have a way to help Colomba get her revenge." Shadow cocks her head to the side in confusion.

"But I thought that Colomba refused to receive superpowers from you. How can you help her get her revenge?" I smile even more deeply.

"Colomba may not want my help, but I know somebody else who will. Transform me into the Crow. I have some work to do." Shadow nods her head before she opens her wings and starts flying in a circle around me, she keeps going faster until she is nothing more than darkness around me. I close my eyes and in an instant she is gone and I am now the Crow. I smile as I close my eyes and whisper in the empty room, "Shadow, find Rosie."

Shadow goes through the hallways, but she can sense that Rosie isn't here. She is not inside the school. Even though we know this we keep searching. I think I know one place she might be. I have heard that the school pays her to take care of the plants in the courtyard during her free period. I bet that they only do that because they feel bad, knowing that they can't do anything to help her with her bully problem, so instead they give her a job. How sad, but she won't have to worry about that much longer. I will make sure that she will get the revenge she deserves.

Shadow passes right through the door leading into the courtyard and just as I thought, Rosie is kneeling there among the neat flowerbeds. She is pulling some weeds near a rose bush, being careful not to harm any of the other flowers and plants. Shadows flies straight into her heart and I introduce myself.

Hello Rosie.

Rosie sits up straight and looks around herself with fear. When she sees that she is alone she closes her eyes and I can feel the tears forming.

"No, I'm not crazy like the other kids said. Mommy said I wasn't crazy so I'm not." She whispers this to herself to try and give herself some comfort.

It is alright Rosie; you are not crazy. I am the Crow and I am here to help you.

Knowing that she isn't hearing voices in her head, Rosie is now completely calm.

"So you want to give me superpowers like all those other kids so that I can get revenge on the bullies, right?" I smile to myself.

Exactly. I think we can work well together. You seem to understand me very well and you have no misgivings about me.

"No, make them all stop hurting me and I will do anything you say." I chuckle to myself. I should have used Rosie from the start. She knows what she wants and is willing to do what it takes to get it.

As you wish.

As Rosie sets her hands down into the earth, the roots of the plants she had so lovingly cared for start creeping out of the ground to begin wrapping around her fingers and arms. It is as if they are creating a shield around her, protecting her from the world that has hurt her far too many times.

Even though most people would be freaking out if they saw this, Rosie is happy. She is happy because, to her, it feels as if her friends are coming out to embrace her. They are giving back the love that she has always shown them. Her lips pull up into a vengeful smile as the roots and vines begin to cover her face. When the vines have covered her entire body I know that she is ready. This school now has one more thing to fear, one more person they should never have hurt.

<u>Chapter Nineteen</u>
Colomba-
The Black Iris

The entire classroom is silent as everyone works on an assignment that the teacher just passed out. My hair is still dripping some water onto my desk and paper, but I try to ignore it. I know that if I start thinking about what happened earlier then I might start crying again. The teacher was annoyed that I came in a bit late, I don't want them even more annoyed by having me cry in their class. It wouldn't help me anyway; everyone would just laugh at me like they have been for the past few weeks. They have no sympathy for me, my tears would only make things worse for me. My heart breaks when I think about how everyone laughed at me earlier when Angela sprayed that water in my face. Why were they so mean to me? I haven't done anything bad to anybody here. Why were they so mean to someone who hasn't done anything to them? Why do people not make any sense?

As I stare down at my paper I notice something strange. The light in the room is fading and it is fading fast. Looking out the window, I see something that sends a chill down my spine. Vines are creeping up from the ground and covering the window faster than any plant has ever grown. Standing up from my chair, I back away from the window in horror. The other students notice my strange behavior, but it doesn't take them long to realize why I am acting so weird. They all glance outside to see that the windows are now completely covered by the plants. All of the students leap away from the window as the vines crash through the glass as if they are reaching out for us.

"Everyone move into the hallway! Get away from the windows!" Everybody follows my instructions and they all run out of the room like a stampede of cows. I follow at the end of the crowd, my heart racing as I watch the vines getting closer and closer to me. When everyone else has left the room, I slam the door behind me just as one of the plants was about to reach my ankle.

Apparently, the other classes are having the same problem since the hallway is now filled with people while some of the students and teachers grab whatever they can to block the doors. They're probably trying to keep the plants from getting to us in the halls. A few people are trying to open a door down the hall that leads outside, but it is blocked on the outside by plants too just like the windows. Something in the back of my mind warns me that the entire school has now been covered by these strange plants.

"This is all your fault isn't it?!" I look behind me to see Angela. She is looking right at me and the entire hallway has gone silent to listen to her. Everyone is listening and paying attention to her, just the way Angela likes it. She is pointing an accusing finger at me and I can feel my hands tightening into fists at my side.

"What are you talking about Angela?" I try to keep my voice calm, but a little growl makes its way into my tone. Angela scoffs at me as if I am being silly before she marches right in front of me so that she is practically yelling in my face.

"All of this stupid! You got your boyfriend, the Crow, to do all of this so that you could help him take over the school! You want all of us to suffer because you are evil just like him!" For the first time in my life I actually want to hit her. I've never been so angry that I've wanted to be violent toward someone, but Angela has finally pushed me to that point. I take a deep breath to calm myself since I know that hitting her won't solve anything.

"Angela, I have been telling all of you guys for the past few weeks that I'm not one of the Crow's followers. I've said that a million times, but none of you have ever believed me! I did not cause any of this!" Angela puts her hands on her hips.

"Well I don't think-" She never got to finish that sentence. I caught sight of something really quickly moving toward us and I pushed her out of the way just in time so that she wasn't hit by a massive vine that had been shooting straight at her. I may have pushed her out of the way, but I didn't move fast enough to get myself out of the way. The vine struck me right in the chest and sent me sailing through the air and landing on the floor in a crumpled heap.

Wheezing in my attempt to breathe, I lift myself up to a sitting position on the ground, but nobody comes over to help me up. They are all too busy staring in horror at what is standing by itself at the other end of the hallway. For some reason it is very dark at that end of the hallway. As we watch whatever it is slowly making its way toward us we find out why it's so dark over there. As it moves vines shoot forward and smash into the lights in the ceiling, making them shatter in a shower of glass and sparks. It moves closer and closer to the massive group of students and teachers who are frozen in fear. I want to scream, to tell them all to run, but I can barely breathe after being hit so hard.

When the mysterious creature is only around twenty feet away from us the entire hall full of people seems to take in a gasp of horror all at once. Standing in front of us is what looks like a human in shape and form but is completely made up of plants. It looks as if someone trimmed a plant in the shape of a teenage girl, like how people cut bushes into animals and weird shapes. Some of the vines making up the creature are a green that's so dark it almost looks black, very strange for a plant. The creature's long yellow hair is made up of a mass of small yellow flowers on thin vines and its blue eyes seem to be some kind of flower as well. The blue flower eyes glance down at the ground, as if the plant person doesn't want to look at any of us. I am confused by this, but I have no time to think about that since the creature raises its arms and more vines shoot out from the darkness behind it and start attacking people. The stillness of the crowd is shattered as everyone runs away from this strange creature, screaming in terror, but nobody stops to help me.

I try to pick myself up quickly, but I still feel too weak. The creature moves closer and stops right beside me. My heart seems to beat so quickly that I'm afraid it will pop out of my chest. The creature's strange eyes glance at me for a moment before it moves off down the hallway. I stare after it in surprise. That thing just completely ignored me? It was willing to try and attack Angela and scare everyone half to death but not even do anything to me? I'm so confused.

What I am not confused by though is that this is definitely the work of the Crow and I am going to have to stop whatever that thing was as Silver Dove. Well now I guess I have to transform into Silver Dove to save all of the people that hate me. Fate, you are so mean to me. Why can't you go pick on somebody else for a change?

Running through the halls, I can't seem to find any place without other people running around me. I need to find a place where I can be alone so nobody will realize who I really am. As I turn down another hallway I run straight into someone. I fall flat on my butt, sending a wave of pain through me in my already pain filled body from that vine smack earlier.

"Oh my gosh, Colomba are you alright?" I glance up in surprise, my pain forgotten, as I look into the face of Luis. He holds out his hands to me to help me up, and I accept them. He lifts me back up to my feet very easily. He's a lot stronger than I expected. He carefully examines me as he repeats his question, "Are you alright?"

I don't get it. Luis is here. I thought that he was the Crow, but he's standing right in front of me right now even though one of the Crow's little minions is running around and causing mayhem. So, Luis must not be the Crow then. I was wrong. Guilt overpowers me as I look into my friend's face. I blamed him for something he didn't do just because of something someone else told me. How could I be so heartless? Everybody has been doing that to me for weeks, yet I did the exact same thing to one of my best friends. What is wrong with me? Luis looks down at me expectantly and I realize that he is still waiting for an answer to his question.

"Yes, yes I'm alright." He smiles down at me.

"Good, now come on. We have to find a safe spot to hide while we wait for everything to calm down." Without giving a moment to respond, he takes me by the hand and starts leading me down the hall. Wow. Luis is being very brave right now. He's trying to protect me in this time of danger even though I had been so mean to him not too long ago. He isn't even showing any fear. I am actually pretty impressed. Luis is usually such a shy guy. This is completely unexpected.

Wait, no, I can't let him lead me somewhere. I need to go and transform into Silver Dove and stop that strange plant person before somebody gets hurt. My only problem is how do I get away from Luis? I don't want to just yank my hand out of his grip and run away or else he will chase after me to try make sure that I'm okay. I also know that I can't just keep following him or else he will take me someplace like an empty classroom and he won't leave my side. I need to do something now or else I will never get away, but what?

Thankfully, fate seems to finally give me a break since fate answers that question for me. I manage to push Luis out of the way just in time before another one of those crazy vines got too close to him. He falls to the floor while I run in the opposite direction with the vine trailing after me.

I run as far and as fast as I can away from the freaky vine and head into a janitor's closet. Thankfully, I don't find anybody else hiding there. I am all alone. I wait for a minute for the vine to pass by the door before I step into action. Placing my hand on the Dove Pin on my chest, I say the magic words, "Peaceful warrior."

The dark room is immediately flooded with light and I close my eyes to keep the light from hurting my eyes. Usually when I am transforming I feel excited, but not today. Today I can only feel miserable. It's hard to be excited when you know you have to save a bunch of people that hate you. I open my eyes to find myself as Silver Dove. My large wings are cramped in this small closet. When I try to open the door to get out, my wings get stuck since they are too big to fit through the slim doorway. Groaning under my breath, I step back as far as I can in the tiny closet and run to the door, leaping at the last second, turning over in midair so that I go through it sideways so that my wings can fit through. I open my wings just as I am about to hit the ground and I take off into the air down the hallway. When people see me flying through the halls that are beginning to be taken over by the crazy fast growing vines, they cheer, happy to know that I will be saving them once again.

Oh yeah, you cheer for me now when only an hour ago you were laughing at me. A dark feeling I am unfamiliar with overshadows me as I fly over everyone. It takes me a minute to realize what it is, hatred. My eyes grow wide behind my mask when I realize that. I actually feel that badly about the other kids in my school? What is wrong with me? I have never hated anybody in my life, but when I look down at the people below me I can't describe how I feel any other way than hatred. This is what must have happened to make the Crow as filled with hate as he is. He must have gotten picked on so long and so mercilessly that hatred just grew in him. As I try to hold down the hatred in me I suddenly understand the Crow. I understand why he is so angry, but I will still never join him. I may not like the people I am about to try and help, but I will always try to do the right thing and right now the right thing would be to end whatever the Crow is trying to do now with that weird plant person.

Flying around several corners, I search for the plant person. It doesn't take me long to realize that all of the strange plants that are slowly creeping across the floor and walls seem to be coming from one general direction. I go to where the plants seem to be coming from and almost fly straight into the plant person. The only thing that prevented me from slamming into her was that she (or her weird plants) must have sensed me coming since a large vine shot out and smacked me out of the air and into a row of lockers, as if I was nothing more than a fly being swatted.

Groaning softly, I pick myself up just in time to see another vine coming at me to hit me again. Faster than I thought I could, I unsheathed my sword and slashed at the vine, cutting it apart before it could even touch me. As soon as my sword cut through the vine the plant person let out a scream of absolute horror.

"You hurt my friend!!" Wait… friend? The plant person waves her hands forward toward me, as if directing someone. Who that someone is is quickly explained. More vines shoot out at me, but my sword just keeps hacking away at them while the plant person continues to scream in terror as their "friends" keep getting cut away by me. When I cut away the last one, I glare at the strange figure in front of me.

"Who are you?!" The plant person balls up the tangle of vines that makes up their hands into tight fists.

"I am the Black Iris!" Iris? Calling the plants her friends and naming herself after an iris, the same kind of flower that someone told me recently is their favorite? There is no question who this plant person really is.

"Rosie, what are you doing?" She actually looks up at me for a moment before averting her eyes down again.

"How did you know it's me?"

"I just do alright. Why are you doing this Rosie? You are a good person. Why are you scaring people?" She pauses as if she is listening to someone silently giving her orders, and I think I have an idea who that person is.

"I'm doing this because I have to."

"You don't have to do anything Rosie. You don't have to do what the Crow tells you. You can walk away from this and everything will be alright like before." She scowls at me.

"Everything wasn't alright before! It was terrible! People always hurt me, always bugging me. They all called me a freak and an idiot, and they hurt my friends just to hurt me. They deserve to be just as scared as they have made me all this time." While she was talking, I didn't realize that another one of her vines was sneaking up behind me. Now it is too late. The vine wraps around my leg and slams me against the lockers, over and over again. In between getting thrown against the wall, I try to swing my sword at the vine, but it gets knocked out of my hand as I slam into the locker. I try to call it back to me, but the vines thickly cover it, blocking it from coming back.

The vine throws me down the hall. I land so hard on one of my wings that I know it would have broken if I didn't have my power of invincibility. I tumble across the floor until I am brought to a stop by hitting against a classroom door. I quickly pick myself up, knowing that she hasn't given up yet. Thank goodness I got up when I did since a huge vine is now coming straight at me, directed at my face. I quickly move out of the way, but only slightly. I move away just enough that the vine misses me, but still close enough to strike back. I lift my hand and use it to chop down on the vine, like the martial artist I am breaking a wooden board. The vine snaps in two, the broken piece falling to the floor and slithering there like a confused snake. The Black Iris yells out in anguish, seeing me harm one of her friends again.

Three more vines shoot out at me. I dodge the first two by a hair, but the third strikes me in the center of my face, sending me flying backward into the wall. This time I don't have the time to pick myself up before she gets me. One of her vines wraps around my leg and then encompasses me all the way up to my chest before I even have time to react. The vine drags me across the floor, my helmet making a terrible scraping sound across the floor tiles, making me wince because I can't cover my ears since the vine has my arms trapped against my body.

The vine drags me until I am at the Black Iris' feet. Then the vine lifts me up so that I am face to face with her.

"You hurt my friends. For that, and everything you have done against the Crow, you will pay." The vine around me slowly begins to tighten, making it harder and harder to breathe. I try to wiggle around to try and escape, but only one hand is free and it is not free enough to really do anything. I look around myself to hopefully find some way to escape, but there is nothing. I glance down and see something that brings a little bit of hope in me.

"Rosie, what kind of flower is that?" Her

rage fades for a moment as she looks at the little white flower I am pointing to with my one free hand on the vine she is standing on.

"That is a bellis perennis, a common European species of daisy. It is also known as the English or lawn daisy and is a perennial flower." I smile at her even though the vine around me is still crushing my ribs.

"Now would an idiot be able to tell me that?" She stares at me, completely shocked by my words. "Rosie, you can tell anyone about any type of plant. An idiot cannot do that. You are different than most people, that is alright. It makes you a more interesting person. You are not stupid just because you are different. It just means that you think in a different way than most people." Her hands clench into fists at her side.

"Everyone always talks to me as if I don't understand. I understand what they say! Just because I'm autistic everyone thinks I'm stupid! I'm not! Why can't they see that I understand?!" The vine around me tightens in her anger and I have to bite my lip to keep myself from crying out.

"If they don't understand you then that's their problem! It doesn't mean that you have the problem! You are the way you are meant to be, and I know that there will be many people who will love you for who you are, not what they wish you to be! You are not an idiot! You are beautiful just the way you are!" The vine around me weakens its grip as the Black Iris lowers her head in guilt.

"You're right. I'm sorry." She doesn't say anymore, but nothing more is needed. All of the vines and other plants she had created rush over to her and wrap around her in what looks like a massive cocoon. A blinding light emanates from the giant mass of plants and I close my eyes. When I open them again the only thing standing in front of me is Rosie, back as her usual self. The two of us glance at each other and I nod at her, giving her a little smile. She looks away from me awkwardly, but I know that it's alright. That's just the way she is.

All around us the school is falling apart. The windows are broken from when she had the vines smash through them. All of the lights aren't working because she smashed those too, and papers and other debris litters the ground. It is a huge mess, but I can fix that easily. Placing my hand over the dove emblem on my armor, I say the magic words, "Bring peace little dove."

The dove on my armor flies off my chest and into the air. It is glowing in the darkness of the hallway, like a lantern in a dark cave. It flies close to the ceiling and begins to glow so brightly that I close my eyes. When the light has faded, I open my eyes again to reveal the school the same as it was only an hour or two ago. Before the Black Iris attacked.

Glancing down, I notice a single sheet of paper laying on the ground beside my foot. Bending down, I pick it up and smile when I see what it is. Turning back to Rosie, I hand her the paper as I give her a gentle smile. Written across the top line of the paper is "My One- Hundred Favorite Flowers". She smiles when she sees that it is her list.

"Thank you, Silver Dove."

"You're very welcome Rosie, and don't worry. I really do think that things will get better for you." I open up my wings and take off down the hall. People come out of their hiding spots to cheer for me as I fly by. My heart aches when I think about how I had felt about them when I was flying over to face the Black Iris, about how I hated them. Right now, they act like I am the greatest hero to ever walk across the face of the earth, but when I am my normal self they push me and treat me like I am worse than nothing. I don't know what I should feel toward them. All I know is that right now my heart is aching in my chest and I don't think it will stop, not for a very long time.

Chapter Twenty
Luis-
What Now

I pace back and forth across the bathroom floor, thinking carefully while Shadow stares at me curiously. Her face remains emotionless. I'm not sure if that's because she's a bird and can't show emotions like people or not, but whatever.

"Are you going to state what is worrying you out loud or am I supposed to guess?" Shadow asks me sarcastically. I stop pacing as I close my eyes and sigh.

"I can't believe it ended that quickly. This was the shortest battle of any of my soldiers so far. I don't know what went wrong. Rosie seemed so determined to do what I wanted, but then she changed her mind just like all the others. I was hoping that this would be the last one." Shadow flies off of the bathroom sink counter and lands on my shoulder.

"I believe that all of us are hoping that each time will be the last." I think she's implying that I should just surrender or something, but she doesn't give me a chance to ask. "Let us not forget about something good that has come out of this. Since Colomba saw you as your usual self during the attack she probably now thinks that you are not the Crow anymore." I smile when I realize that she is right.

"Of course, I nearly forgot about that." I lower my head though when I realize what I wasn't able to do with the Black Iris that I had hoped for. What little happiness I felt when Shadow mentioned that quickly fades as I state my major failure with this mission.

"Well what am I going to do now? They're still going to hurt her. I failed. I wanted to make sure that they would stop making fun of Colomba, but I failed. The Black Iris failed, and I failed too. I've let her down." Shadow uses her beak to push away my bangs that are hanging in my face. No matter how badly I feel this makes me feel a little better. Whenever she does this it almost feels as if I have a mother to comfort me. My mom and dad died when I was a baby, so this is kind of the only time I've ever had someone like a mother to me. It is a wonderful feeling.

"I wouldn't say that Master. Things may work out differently than you expect. If what I think will happen is correct, then Colomba will be perfectly fine." I look at her, trying to smile with hope.

"Do you really think so?" Shadow nods at me.

"Yes, even if you didn't do anything I think that things would have quieted down for her anyway. She is a very sweet and gentle girl. She wouldn't want to be a part of any kind of battle with anybody. She wouldn't take sides. She may have cheered for one side, but she would have never helped in the fight. Everyone else would have realized this sooner or later, and people would start treating her like they had before. I think what you have done though may have speeded that up that process. Perhaps by tomorrow things may be a lot different for Colomba. I truly believe that things will be alright for her." I stroke her feathers with the tips of my fingers.

"I really hope you're right. I don't want to ever see her cry again. It nearly killed me watching it earlier." Shadow nods her head.

"I understand. It is always a painful experience to watch someone you care for being hurt." I lower my head, not wanting her to see the pain in my eyes.

"Yeah, it really does." Outside the bathroom I can hear the other students filing out of the classrooms they had been hiding in and heading to the buses and cars outside, waiting to take them home. "I guess it's time to go home Shadow." She nods.

"I guess so." Without another word she flies off my shoulder and straight into the medal on my shirt. As soon as she has disappeared into the medal, I cover the medal with my hoodie and head out the door to join the massive crowd.

While I walk through the crowd I look at all the people around me. I watch them all as they talk excitedly about what just happened with the

Black Iris and Silver Dove. They all chat with their friends while I am all alone. I always feel the loneliest when I am alone in a crowd. I can only hope that Colomba isn't feeling the same way. I can only hope that Shadow is right, and that things will work out well for her. I do have my doubts though. After everything in have lived through I doubt that people can turn around and stop hurting someone and be kind to them again. I don't believe that people will give each other a second chance, even when they find out that they were wrong. Most people are terrible, always beating down the good people who have never done anything bad to them.

When I look at them all, I have no hope.

<u>Chapter Twenty- One</u>
Colomba-
A Happy Ending
For the Both of Us

.   The night has passed and a new day has dawned since my battle with the Black Iris. I enter through the front doors of my school feeling hopeful, not hopeful that things will be better for me, but hopefully better for Rosie. I guess, in a way, I have given up hoping that things will get better for me. Everyone thinks that I am helping the Crow and I have tried to tell them that I'm not, but nobody listens. They will keep believing that until I graduate from this school or someone convinces them otherwise, but I don't think that the second one is going to happen any time soon.

Searching through the halls before class officially starts, I easily find who I am looking for. Rosie is placing a large poster on the wall, several more posters rolled up in her arms. I run over to her, eager to talk to her.

"Hi Rosie." Rosie glances at me for only a moment before returning her gaze to the poster she is taping to the wall.

"Hi Colomba."

"How are you doing after everything that happened yesterday?"

"I'm doing a lot better." I wait for her to say more, but I smile when I realize she won't. One thing I have learned about her since I have met her is that if you want to know something specific you have to ask it very directly since she might not understand what is implied from a question.

"How are things getting better?" Rosie points to the poster that she just finished taping to the wall. I look at it for the first time and realize what it is. On the poster it is telling everyone that a new club will be forming, a gardening club.

"After what happened yesterday the principal called me in and told me that, after everything that has happened to me with the bullying from the other kids, then I could start a gardening club here at the school. They even have a spot in the back of the school that they will be clearing up so we can build a garden. The first meeting is next week after school on Friday if you want to come." My heart seems to fill with joy at her words.

"I would love to join your club. If you're in it I know that I will learn a lot." Rosie seems to perk up knowing that I will be joining her club and that I am happy that she will be leading it.

"Thank you… Silver Dove." My eyes grow wide as Rosie looks me in the eyes for the first time ever and smiles. My racing heart slows down when I realize that my secret is safe with her. I have helped her; to repay me she will keep my secret.

"I told you that you're not an idiot Rosie. You seem to be smarter than everyone else in this school. Nobody else has figured it out yet besides you." She looks away from my gaze as she smiles proudly.

"I won't tell anybody who you are. I'll see you at the first meeting then." She walks away, almost skipping in her joy. I watch her leave for a moment, feeling overjoyed that I have helped her become more confident and happy with herself.

I watch her for a moment, feeling proud and content. I let myself enjoy this feeling, knowing that it may be the only real happiness I will have today. I walk straight to my locker to pick up a few books for my first classes. I try not to look at anybody around me, knowing that they might say or do something mean to me because of the rumors.

Opening up my locker, after I take out the books I need I pull a small object out of my bag and place it on a shelf in the locker. I smile up at the little figure I had made from a piece of my broken practice weapon. I had just finished carving and painting it last night. Sitting peacefully on the top shelf of my locker is a small wooden dove. I have carved a few figures before, but I think that this one has to be the best. It practically looks like it's alive, as if it could fly off my locker shelf at any moment. My martial arts teacher, Jeff, was the one to teach me how to carve wood. He's full of odd little talents that he likes to pass on to anyone willing to learn. I take one last look at my little dove before I close my locker and start heading to class.

Walking down the halls by myself, people look

away when they notice me. They have been doing this ever since what happened with the Sprinter, but this time it is a bit different. Usually they look away out of fear or hatred. Today they are looking away with something I don't really understand. Is the look on their faces… guilt? What on earth is going on? Do they really feel guilty about something related to me? Why are they feeling guilty when everyone still thinks I'm a monster? I stop walking when I hear someone calling out my name from behind me.

"Hey Colomba, can we talk to you?" Turning around I am facing several people that I had considered to be my friends before everyone started picking on me, then they abandoned me. When I look at them I feel both angry and happy. Angry that they abandoned me, yet happy that they are talking to me again.

"Sure of course." One of them, Aaron, speaks up, looking down at his feet awkwardly, as if he is nervous about what he plans on saying.

"We just wanted to say that we're sorry that we treated you so badly. We all know now that you aren't on the same side as the Crow. If you were then you wouldn't have saved Angela earlier when that vine tried to grab her, especially after what she did to you earlier the other day. Do you forgive us?" I smile at him, holding back the tears of joy that threaten to fall down my face.

"Of course I do. I understand. If I thought that somebody was on the side of the Crow I would be a bit afraid of them too." I open out my arms and they all join me in a massive group hug. They all start talking to me, asking me how I've been and telling me that they're so happy that they are talking to me again.

As I listen to them talk I have a huge grin on my face because I think I understand what is going on. This is the end of everyone picking on me. I have no doubt that the news of what I did for Angela during all of that craziness will spread throughout the school and nobody will ever think that I'm siding with the Crow ever again. My pain and misery are over. I am finally free. For the first time in a very long time I am free.

I head to class with them, smiling with the first real smile I have had in several weeks. It feels so nice just to have someone to talk to on the way to class. To not let someone be lonely can be one of the greatest things you can ever do for somebody. It lets them know that they are not alone.

<u>Chapter Twenty- Two</u>
Luis-
Disappearing for
the Moment

As I make my way to my first class I carefully scan the crowd like I always do to make sure that none of my usual bullies are near me so that they can try to do one of their usual pranks. Not too long ago, I wasn't paying attention and one of them pulled down my pants in front of everyone. Thankfully, after having this happen so many times to me, I have developed fast reflexes and I managed to pull them back up quickly before too many people saw my boxers. Most people would probably think that it's really strange to be used to that, but I am. There is no other way of saying this without it being a lie. I am used to the embarrassment and torture that they put me through all the time.

It's been like this almost every day since Kindergarten. I wish I could change it faster, but one day one of my plans as the Crow will work out and I will never have to watch my back like this again. I smile for a moment at the thought of that, but I let the smile fade quickly since I know that one of my bullies might see it and want to do something to me to make the smile disappear.

Turning a corner, I stop in surprise when I see something I didn't expect to see for a very long time. Colomba is smiling, surrounded by friendly faces who are smiling back at her with true affection for her. What is happening here? I glance around her to make sure that this isn't some kind of prank; that they aren't just pretending to be friendly to her so that one of them can catch her when she isn't expecting it and do something cruel to her. I watch and I wait, but nothing happens as they continue walking down the hall. They're all chatting happily as if none of them had been teasing and avoiding her just the other day.

When I look at Colomba her smile is not fake. She is showing them true friendliness. She has forgiven them completely for what they all did to her. Truthfully, if I was in her shoes, I would have found it very difficult to forgive them. I may not have even done it at all. That's probably the biggest difference between the two of us. She has a bigger heart and is willing to forget the mistakes and pain in the past while I cannot. I am always trapped in the misery of what has already happened. Even though this sad thought keeps circling around my mind, I still smile, seeing that she is happy and loved once again. I'm happy that Shadow was right. I'm disappointed that the Black Iris didn't fix all of the bullying in the school like I had hoped, but she did do this one good thing for me. For that, I am happy.

I'm about to walk away when someone steps in front of Colomba, almost walking into her. The group around her falls silent as they all stare at Angela with a worried expression as she stares at Colomba. For a moment all is silent, as if Angela is thinking about saying something. My heart jumps in my chest when I think that she might actually thank Colomba for saving her during the attack yesterday. She opens her mouth, as if she is going to speak, but quickly snaps it shut and walks away with her nose in the air. I almost laugh at this show of extreme pride. What a snobby little brat! She can't even thank a person who saved her from a plant creature's wrath! What is wrong with that girl?

I walk down the hall to head to my first class, hiding my smile again as the teacher talks and I take notes. When the bell rings, signaling the end of class, I rush out the door to head to my second period, eager to get there since I share that class with Colomba. Since I practically ran to the classroom, I am the first to arrive, so I sit down at my desk and wait for her. It doesn't take her long to come into the room with a thousand-watt smile directed at me.

"Luis, you're not going to guess what happened?!" I smile back at her.

"What?"

"Everyone saw what happened during the Black Iris' attack when I saved Angela from getting hit by that vine, and now everyone has finally realized that I'm not on the Crow's side. It's finally going to end! Everyone is going to stop messing with me!"

"Congratulations! I'm so happy for you."
We talk for a few minutes before class starts and the
teacher talks about something that I have a hard
time paying attention to. I am too happy for what
has happened with Colomba to even think about
school work.

The rest of the day passes by uneventfully,
and Colomba and I talk with each other as we walk
to the bus after the final bell rings. We joke around
as we make our way through the crowded hallway,
but the lighthearted atmosphere completely changes
when Colomba's tone suddenly gets very serious.

"Hey Luis." I look down at Colomba who
is staring down at the ground in embarrassment.

"What is it Colomba?"

"I just wanted to tell you that I'm sorry. I
should have believed you when you said that you
weren't the Crow. I'm sorry I blamed you for all of
that. Can you forgive me?" When I look down at
her guilty face I can't help but feel guilty too. I have
lied to her. I have made her think that I'm not the
Crow, even though I am, because I want to keep her
friendship. Is that such a bad thing, to lie so you can
keep a friend? Isn't it understandable? Isn't it
understandable to do something a little bit wrong so
that you can keep one of the only good things in
your life? I smile down at her, wanting to tell her
the truth, but knowing I can't.

"Of course, I forgive you." When she
smiles at me it feels as if all of the pain that has
been buried inside of me all my life disappears. She
surprises me by wrapping her arms around me in a
warm hug. I hug her back, thinking that this has to

be one of the greatest moments of my life.

The two of us walk out of the school together to head to our bus. As we walk out the front doors I notice someone familiar leaning against the wall as if waiting for someone, Alex. Colomba and I pass by him and his eyes grow wide when he sees that Colomba is still willingly letting me hang out with her despite the rumors he spread about me.

There is also another look on his face that confuses me for a moment before I realize what it is, disappointment. In a flash I understand why he is feeling this way. He was hoping that he could walk with Colomba down the hall to her bus, he wanted to spend time with her, but I have taken his place. Me, the guy he thinks of as a complete loser, is talking with the girl he wants and she is actually enjoying my company. She and Alex had been spending a lot more time together when I had tried to avoid her in fear that she might get hurt by Alex, and now he is realizing that his time of being her favorite between the two of us is now over.

Colomba gives him a simple, friendly wave and a smile as we walk past him, leaving him alone. I smile at him too, but not in a friendly way like Colomba. I smirk at him, showing off my victory. I smile knowing that I have beaten him again when it comes to having Colomba's attention. He may have been beating me for a while recently, but that is over, and I have won this major battle. Alex glares at me as I turn my attention back to Colomba and we chat as we get onto the bus to head home. She and I, as well as Nat, talk the entire way until it is my time to leave them.

The bus pulls in front of my uncle's antique shop and I jump off with a spring in my step as I head straight into the apartment above the shop. I spend the rest of the afternoon doing some of my chores and playing a few games on my computer. When night falls, I pull out the sketchbook with all of the drawings of my soldiers. I flip to the first empty page and begin to sketch out the Black Iris. I pay close attention to the vines that make up her body, not really sure how to draw that since I have never drawn anything like that before. I never even thought of having a plant person until I decided to make Rosie my soldier. With her love of plants it just seemed like the logical choice.

She had done well; I think to myself as I sketch out her face and the strange flower eyes. She was really terrifying. When I had transformed back into my usual self during the attack so I could convince Colomba that I'm not the Crow, I was afraid even though I knew she wouldn't attack me. I gave her a long list of people she was not allowed to attack. I was on that list along with Colomba and Nat, as well as several other bullied kids that I don't want to get hurt. I made sure that the list was long so that she wouldn't be able to find out which one of the people on it is really the Crow just in case she realized that I was leaving my Crow form and being my normal self. She never saw me face to face while I was in my normal form, but her vines could tell that I was her ally, so they didn't attack me.

I'm so glad that she didn't seem to catch on about who I am. My plans would be ruined if she were to spread that around. The other students in this school would probably destroy me if they found out who I really am. I stop drawing for a second when I think about that. Would they hurt me if they found out or would they run away in fear? For my own sake, I hope they run away.

When the drawing is finished I stare at it with joy. The Black Iris may not have ended the bullying in the school, which is my overall goal, but she did accomplish what I had I set out to do, help Colomba. Because of what happened during the attack nobody believes that she is on my side anymore and they are treating her just as kindly as they did before. Also, Colomba no longer believes that I am the Crow and is hanging out with me again. Even though in many ways the Black Iris failed, in my eyes she succeeded. She gave me what Colomba and I wanted. I think that I can count this as one of my first real victories as the Crow.

Glancing over at the alarm clock next to my bed, I can see that it is getting late. I get ready for bed and pull away the covers. As I lie down in my bed, getting ready to fall asleep, I think about everything that has happened. I think about what happened the other day with Rosie, about how Colomba finally decided to believe me and not Alex and became my friend again, but more than anything I think about what happened before all of that. I think about how everyone picked on Colomba because of me, because they thought that she was on the same side as the Crow. I close my eyes and clench my fists at the thought. I really was responsible for that, and I think it will be a long time before I can forgive myself for it.

As the minutes tick by on the clock beside my bed I think of something that might be for the best. Maybe it would be good for the Crow to take a little break. I should give myself more time to plan things out and practice more with my powers. Every time I have given someone powers so far I kind of made the decision on the spot. I need to think things out better or else I will always be seen as the bad guy. I want to be the good guy here.

I want everyone I go to school with now to look back and think of me as the hero, someone they can tell their kids about with pride, not hatred. Maybe I need to give everyone some time to remember just how bad all of the bullying is in this school so that they can remember that I am here to help end the bullying while Silver Dove will do nothing to help them. I want to give them time to miss me before I can come back. Maybe once things get worse with my absence they will miss the Crow and beg me to come back.

Yes, that's what I need to do. Wait for them to miss me and then they will want me back. They will beg for the Crow to save them and maybe I will, but maybe I won't.

Eliza Scalia is a therapist who has a Masters degree in Clinical Mental Health from Troy University. She enjoys reading, writing, and needlework, as well as hanging out with her pet cat, Dusty. Eliza has been writing since she was in middle school and has self- published the Death's Assistant series for young adults.